BLOOD MOON RISING

A TALE OF TERROR FOR THE 21st CENTURY

UNIVERSAL STUDIOS MONSTERS

THE WOLF MAN™

By Larry Mike Garmon

SCHOLASTIC INC.

New York   Toronto   London   Auckland   Sydney
Mexico City   New Delhi   Hong Kong   Buenos Aires

No part of this publication may be reproduced in whole or in part, or stored in a retrieval system, or transmitted in any form or by any means, electronic, mechanical, photocopying, recording, or otherwise, without written permission of the publisher. For information regarding permission, write to Scholastic Inc., Attention: Permissions Department, 555 Broadway, New York, NY 10012.

ISBN 0-439-20847-5

© 2001 Universal Studios Publishing Rights, a division of Universal Studios Licensing, Inc. All rights reserved. The Universal Studios Monsters are trademarks and copyrights of Universal Studios.
THE WOLF MAN is a trademark and copyright of Universal Studios.
Published by Scholastic Inc.
SCHOLASTIC and associated logos are trademarks and/or registered trademarks of Scholastic Inc.

Designed by Peter Koblish

12 11 10 9 8 7 6 5 4 3 2 1 0   1 2 3 4 5 6/0
Printed in the U.S.A.
First Scholastic printing, August 2001

For Alex, who has brought another reason to smile and laugh into my life.

PROLOGUE
Friday, Twilight

"That's the way to kill those wild wolves!" the carnival barker yelled over the noise of the crowd and the rides that lined the midway. "Three shots; three wolves. You win the little lady a stuffed gorilla." The barker reached up and pulled down a large purple stuffed gorilla with orange hair and a large banana in one hand. Then he turned his attention back to the crowd flowing by his booth. "Step right up! A winner every time . . ."

Don Earl Abernathy laid the small pellet rifle on the counter.

"Oh, Don Earl. Just what I always wanted," Gayle Braddock said as she picked up the gorilla.

"Ah, shucks," Don Earl said in a slow southern drawl, kicking at the ground with one foot. "T'-weren't nuthin'!"

Gayle stood up on tiptoe and kissed him on the cheek. "But ya won it jest fer me," she replied, imitating his drawl.

They looked at each other and laughed.

"Sound like a couple of hicks, don't we?" Don Earl said.

"Well, when in Hick City," Gayle said, shrugging.

"C'm on, let's go on the Whirly-Loop again." Don grabbed Gayle by the hand and started dragging her down the midway.

"No, Don," she protested. "I'm still sick from the last time we rode it."

"That's the coolest ride at the carnival," Don said. "It's like riding around those barrels. You don't get sick riding your horse at breakneck speed around barrels, do you?"

"That's different. I'm in control during a barrel race. All that Whirly-Loop does is toss you up while it spins around and around, then turns upside down and reverses itself. Can't we just walk around and look at the people?" She shot her boyfriend her sweetest smile. *"Please?"*

Don Earl sighed. "Okay. If that's what you want to do."

The midway smelled of dirt, grease, sweat, and deep-fried food. Neon greens, yellows, blues, and reds swirled in the air above each ride. The roar of people shouting, screaming, laughing, and talking mingled with the metallic grinding of gears, while the blare of heavy metal music kept an ominous beat in the background. The smell and the lights and the noise distracted the carnival-goers not just from their daily chores and worries, but also from the rust-colored moon that slowly crept across the dark and cloudless sky.

"Probably just want to show off that buckle you're carrying," Don commented as they strolled along.

"So what if I do? Anything wrong with that?" Gayle challenged him.

"Not that I can see. I don't just have the prettiest girl at the fair, I've got the barrel racing champion to boot." He pulled his black cowboy hat down to the top of his eyebrows, nodding with pride.

Gayle stuck her arm into Don Earl's and the pair continued down the midway. Their day had been filled with excitement at the annual Wales Rodeo and Founders' Day Festival and Carnival. Don had made the finals of the high school bull-wrestling event and was scheduled to compete the next night, the last night of the annual fair and carnival. He was favored to win the event.

Don looked at his girlfriend out of the corner of his eye: Her soft blond hair was luminous in the neon glow of the carnival lights. The half-moon silver earrings he had given her as a birthday present bounced in rhythm to her step. Her blue eyes sparkled with excitement and enjoyment of the evening's festivities.

Tonight was Gayle's night. She had won first place in the high school division of the barrel racing competition, and she'd been selected as rodeo queen as well. She proudly draped her trophy across her right shoulder: a leather belt with a large buckle at one end. The buckle was oval and showed a girl guiding her horse around a barrel in a cloud of dust. It was made of solid silver and was extremely heavy, which is why Gayle had it slung across her shoulder instead of laced through her belt loops. The buckle was so heavy she thought it would rip the loops of her jeans.

The Rodeo and Founder's Day Festival and Carnival was held each October in the rural town of Wales, Florida, a small town just north of Orlando, next to the Ocala National Forest. The town was the hub of a large farming and ranching community in central Florida. The annual rodeo was hugely popular. Winners of each event went on to the state competition and then to the national high school finals. The Ocala Indian Nation ran the annual rodeo and carnival, donating the use of their tribal lands.

"How about a hot dog?" Gayle suggested.

Don Earl's face screwed up into a grimace. "I don't see how you can eat that stuff."

"They're good! Especially with lots of relish, onions, and chili."

Don made a retching sound and bent over as though he were throwing up.

Gayle laughed. "I don't think I've ever met a cowboy who's a vegetarian."

"Just something about eating the flesh of another

animal that doesn't set right with me. Especially cows."

"Cows are ugly," Gayle said with a laugh. "We're doing them a favor by eating them. Besides, aren't you being a little cruel wrestling them in the rodeo?"

"Hey, wrestling them is one thing — eating them is quite another." Don Earl's laugh was deep and warm. Gayle squeezed his arm, pulling herself closer to him. "Besides, you eat all that chili and onions and I'm afraid you can kiss your good-night kiss good-bye!" Don waved his hand in front of his face as though fanning away bad breath.

"That's what you say *now*," Gayle said, elbowing Don.

Don faked a groan and laughed.

"Look, there's a fortune-teller," Gayle said, pointing through the crowd at a lone booth several yards back from the midway. "Let's get our fortunes told."

"Those things are as fake as three-dollar bills."

"Who cares? It'll be fun." Gayle began to pull her boyfriend toward the booth.

"I'm not going to pay five bucks to get a fake fortune," Don protested.

"I'll pay," Gayle said, reaching into her pocket. She pulled out a fifty-dollar bill.

"That's your prize money."

"To do with as I wish," Gayle said with a smile. "And I wish for us to have our fortunes told."

She had to drag Don the remaining ten yards to the entrance of the fortune-teller's tent. It was an old army tent that had been patched and stitched back together. The once dark fabric had faded to a whitish-green. The rusty full moon seemed to have stopped over the tent like a beacon.

Gayle had to get behind her tall, lanky boyfriend and push him through the opening. They spilled into the tent, laughing.

"It is not good to laugh in the house of the spirits," said an old woman sitting behind a table at the opposite end of the tent.

"We're sorry," Gayle said, dropping her smile. "I just had to use a little extra persuasion to get my boyfriend in here."

"He does not believe in the spirits?" the old woman said.

"I don't know," Gayle replied. She turned to Don Earl. "Do you believe in the spirits?"

Don Earl was staring at the old woman. Her hair was gray and her face was brown and wrinkled — deep, fleshy wrinkles that folded over one another. He was used to seeing such worn and leathery faces on the old cowhands who had worked their entire adult lives in the sun and weather. But what caught Don Earl's attention was the woman's right eye. While her left eye was a clear, deep brown, her right was an opaque milky white. It did not move when the left eyed moved. The dead eye remained still. Still and staring at Don Earl.

"She looks just a little younger than dirt," he whispered to Gayle. Gayle elbowed him in the ribs again.

"It is not important that you believe in the spirits," the old woman said. "What is important is that the spirits believe in you. Come." She motioned for the couple to sit in the two seats across from her.

Silently, Don Earl and Gayle sat.

"I am a shaman of the Ocala people." The fortune-teller placed a small fur bag on the table. It cinched with a short leather string at the top.

"Can you tell us our fortune?" Gayle said.

"No. I am not a fortune-teller. I am a shaman. My magic does not tell the fortunes of those who ask. My magic tells of the spirits who are accompanying you on your journey on this earth. The evil spirits and the good spirits."

"Yeah, right," Don Earl said with a smirk.

"*Don!*" Gayle said.

He moved before her elbow could connect with his chest again.

Gayle turned to the Ocala shaman. "Can you break a fifty?" She held out the crisp new bill.

The shaman reached into a pocket of her faded and patched skirt and pulled out a wad of bills. "I am to tell the spirits of one or two?"

"Both of us," Gayle replied with a smile. She winked at Don. Don rolled his eyes and pursed his lips.

The shaman counted out forty dollars in fives

and tens and handed them to Gayle. She snatched the fifty from Gayle, and it and the wad disappeared into her skirt pocket.

"Now, I will tell of the spirits who are trying to destroy you and the spirits who are trying to protect you." The shaman picked up the bag, unstrung the leather tie, and poured the contents — several small bones, a polished stone, a dried clump of dirt, and a feather — onto the table.

"My little brother has a collection like that in his junk drawer," Don Earl said.

"Hush, Don," Gayle said, a stern look on her face. "You don't have a little brother!"

"I will do the unbeliever first," the shaman said, the opaque eye staring at Don. "The tokens of the spirit will tell of his good spirits and evil spirits." She picked up the bones, stone, dirt, and feather and hid them in her clasped hands. She looked at Don Earl and mumbled, her words soft and alien to the couple. Then she tossed the tokens in Don's direction.

The bones, dirt, and stone rolled across the table and stopped inches away from the edge, right in front of Don. The feather floated in the air for a few moments, then landed on one of the bones.

Don Earl sat back in his chair and pushed his hat back on his head, revealing his forehead.

The shaman gasped. Gayle looked up at her. The shaman wasn't looking at the tokens. She was staring at Don Earl.

"You must go," the shaman said, scooping up the tokens and placing them in the fur bag. "You must go quickly. Go home." She rose and started for the entrance. "You must go."

"What's wrong?" Gayle said.

"I'll tell you what's wrong," Don began as they stood up. "We paid ten bucks to get junk thrown at us, and we didn't even get our fortunes told."

The shaman reached into her pocket and pulled out the wad of bills. She grabbed two crumbled fives and threw them at the couple. "You must go now." She held the flap of the tent open for them.

"*This* has been a lot of fun," Don Earl said, sarcastically, picking up the bills.

"What's wrong?" Gayle asked the shaman. "What did you see in the tokens? What spirits did you see?"

"No spirits." The shaman waved her arm for them to leave. "You go now."

"What do you mean, *no spirits*?" Gayle said, her voice rising. "What did you see? You must tell us."

The shaman stood silently in the doorway, nodding and mumbling.

"What did you see?" Gayle begged.

The shaman stared at Don Earl's exposed forehead with the one good, deep brown eye. The dead eye stared into nothingness. She reached up with her hand, a weathered bony finger inching toward Don Earl's forehead.

"Here," the shaman said as her finger touched

his forehead. "Here is the spirit of evil, the spirit of death." Her finger traced an image visible only to herself. "A five-pointed star — the pentagram." She lowered her arm. *"Even a man who is pure in heart and says his prayers by night may become a wolf when the wolfbane blooms and the autumn moon is bright."* The old shaman let the flap of the tent fall. Through the faded green canvas she said in a muffled voice, "Beware the *skinwalker*."

"Let's go, Gayle." Don took his girlfriend by the arm and led her from the tent. They stepped into the night air. Don Earl took a deep breath. "Creepy." They walked away quickly.

"Let's go home, Don," Gayle said. "I'm a little scared."

"She's a sideshow," Don Earl said. "She's paid to scare people. Gets them excited and then they want to eat more and go on more rides. It's a scam."

Gayle turned back to look at the shaman's tent as they walked. The shaman stood in the tent's opening, the light from the tent silhouetting her. Her hands were raised, the palms facing the two teens. Gayle could hear a soft chant.

"Let's go home, Don Earl. *Please?*" She jumped in front of him, stopping him. She looked at him with persuasive blue eyes. *"Please?"*

Don sighed, then he laughed softly. "Sure, if you want to. I'm sorry I acted like such a jerk. I just don't like anybody scaring my favorite gal." He kissed her on the forehead. Gayle smiled and her eyes brightened. "See a pentagram on my fore-head?" he said, removing his hat.

Don Earl stood over six feet tall while Gayle was barely five feet in her boots. Even though Don was leaning down toward her, Gayle still had to stand on tiptoe to get a look at his forehead.

"Nah," she replied, brushing his brow with her hand. "Just some dung from your bull ride." She laughed.

Don put his hat back on. "Funny. I just want to check John Wayne before we leave."

"Okay," Gayle said. "I want to say good night to Miss Prissy."

They headed to the stables where the horses were kept. John Wayne, Don Earl's horse, was at one end of the huge stable building while Gayle's champion mare, Miss Prissy, was housed at the opposite end. The aisle separating the stalls was lit only by three weak lightbulbs suspended from the high ceiling: dim enough to let the horses sleep, and just enough light to keep people from stumbling around.

"I'm just going to make sure that John Wayne has enough oats for the night," Don Earl said as he headed toward the stall.

"And I've got a surprise for Miss Prissy." Gayle pulled a carrot from her hip pocket. She blew a kiss and waved at Don Earl. "I'll miss you." She turned and walked swiftly to Miss Prissy's stall at the opposite end.

Don Earl chuckled softly. He watched her walk partway down the aisle.

"Whoa there, boy," Don said as he entered John Wayne's stall. The horse had backed up against the end of the stall, his head and ears raised, his ears up and alert to the intruder. "It's just me." The horse's head lowered, as did the ears, in recognition of his master. "There, there, nothing to be scared of." He stroked John Wayne's nose. The horse snorted with approval. "I love you, too."

Don Earl grabbed the oats bag hanging on the stall door. It was nearly empty. He headed out of the stall toward the oat bin. He shoveled three scoops of oats into the bag and returned to the stall, hanging the bag over the door so John Wayne could munch as he pleased. He picked up a brush and began stroking the horse's long, slick brown fur. "Gotta look pretty for tomorrow's championship run. Wouldn't be here if it weren't for you, ol' boy."

The horse shook his coat appreciatively. He tilted his head forward and nibbled from the bag.

"Don't overeat. I don't need you throwing up in the arena," Don cautioned.

The horse nodded, munching on a mouthful of oats. Then suddenly he raised his head, his ears at attention. John Wayne whinnied and backed against the end of the stall again, almost knocking Don Earl to the stall floor.

"Whoa there, boy. What's gotten into you?" He

looked into his horse's eyes. The dark orbs were open wide with fear.

"What is it, boy?" Don Earl walked to the stall door and glanced over the top. Perhaps a cat had gotten inside. John Wayne did not like cats. "Nothing here." He looked down the long aisle of stalls. In the dimness, Don Earl could see a stall door at the far end was ajar. Miss Prissy's stall door. That wasn't like Gayle. She wouldn't leave the stall door open.

Don climbed over the door of John Wayne's stall and started down the aisle toward his girlfriend.

"Gayle?" he called out. "Everything okay?" He continued walking down the aisle. "C'mon, Gayle, you know you can't scare me."

He reached the open door and entered the stall. Miss Prissy was on the ground, motionless.

"Gayle?" He looked around. In the dim light, he could see his girlfriend cowering in a corner, her face pale and her eyes wide with fear. Her mouth was opening and closing, but she was making no sound.

Don followed her gaze, straining his eyes to see in the gloom. Miss Prissy lay still. The horse's chest wasn't even rising and falling. Then he smelled it. An unmistakable smell. Growing up on a farm, raising cattle and chickens and other animals, Don Earl was very familiar with the smell of blood — and death.

He started toward the fallen horse but stopped short as a large, dark figure stirred from the dusky corner just behind Miss Prissy.

Don stood with his feet set apart and his fists clenched. "All right, mister. Stand up."

The figure moved and stood. But not on two legs: on four. Even in the dimness of the stall, Don could tell that the dog facing him was large, the largest dog he'd ever seen.

The animal lowered its head. Don gasped as he saw two large red eyes staring at him — like the little red-light lasers some kids at school liked to point at other students.

Don stood between the giant dog and his girlfriend. "Gayle," he began softly, "move slowly to the door." He turned slightly toward Gayle, keeping one eye on the dog. Gayle was not moving. "Please, move slowly." She still hadn't moved. He turned slightly and saw her staring at the dog. "Don't stare at him. Dogs are threatened when you stare at them. Just get up slowly and move behind me to the door. Now, Gayle. Please."

A low guttural growl filled the stall. Don turned his full attention back to the dog. His eyes were fully adjusted to the gloom. Now it was clear that he was facing not a large dog, but a giant wolf. A giant wolf with bloodred eyes. Its black lips were pulled back in an angry snarl.

Don stepped backward. He knelt slowly down

and tugged gently at Gayle's arm. He whispered, "Let's go."

Gayle stood mechanically. Don guided her cautiously back, out of the stall. Gayle moved like a sleepwalker being put back into bed.

The wolf easily stepped over the dead horse and moved closer to the two teens.

Don Earl glanced to his left. Miss Prissy's stall was next to the stable's north entrance. He led Gayle backward toward the opening. The wolf followed, pausing at the stall door.

Suddenly, Don Earl kicked at the opened stall door, slamming the door shut and putting a barrier between them and the giant wolf.

"Run!" he yelled, tugging at Gayle's arm. She obeyed without protest and ran alongside him.

What sounded like distant rolls of staccato thunder came from behind them. Don knew it was the deep, thick growl of the wolf. He also knew that such a large beast could leap the stall door without effort. He hoped that he and Gayle would have enough time to escape.

He heard a loud splintering sound and looked back. The wolf hadn't bothered to jump the stall door. It had crashed though the wood and was bolting toward them at top speed.

Gayle screamed. She, too, was looking back at the wolf. She had finally come out of her horrified trance.

They ran out of the building into the dark blue night with its rust-colored full moon, racing as fast as they could back toward the carnival.

Then something large and heavy struck Don Earl in the back. He had been butted by bulls before, but nothing had ever hit him with such force. He crashed to the ground, the breath knocked out of him. Darkness swam before his eyes, pinpoint flashes of light exploding against the back of his eyeballs. He shook his head and tried to push himself up, but he couldn't feel his arms. Don fell back to the ground. He could see Gayle on the ground a few feet away. She was unconscious. The wolf stood over her, its red eyes focused on the prone girl, jaw dangling open over huge teeth.

"No," Don Earl whispered hoarsely. Feeling returned to his arms. He pushed himself up, his hands searching the ground for a rock, a stick, anything he could use as a weapon.

His hands hit upon a leather strap. He lifted it. To his surprise, it was heavy. Then a silver glint caught his eye. It was the heavy silver belt and buckle that Gayle had won hours earlier.

Don stood up. His legs felt like rubber. He steadied himself and raised the belt over his head.

The wolf's eyes bored into his. It stepped over Gayle and toward Don Earl.

Good, he thought. *Move away from Gayle.*

Don took a step back. The wolf matched him step for step.

The night suddenly seemed bright. The rustiness of the moon had waxed into a blazing red. For the first time Don saw the wolf clearly. It was not like any wolf he had ever seen before. It was huge, at least three feet at the shoulders — the size of a colt. The head was not oblong, like a dog, but more round and full, like a man's. Its red eyes revealed the understanding both of an intelligent beast and a primitive human.

Don had retreated several yards when he heard a moan. He looked past the wolf and saw that Gayle was struggling to get up.

The wolf turned its massive head and it, too, saw the girl moving.

"No!" Don Earl yelled. He ran at the wolf and brought the massive silver buckle down on the beast's head.

The wolf howled in pain and cowered away from Don, its tail between its legs.

Don Earl continued to swing the heavy buckle at the wolf as he circled around it. Now he was between the wolf and Gayle.

The wolf stayed just out of reach of the flailing buckle. It lifted its head. Its ears were pulled back, its dark lips curled over the teeth. It snarled menacingly.

Don's arms grew heavier with each swing of the buckle. He breathed deeply. He continued to move toward the wolf, backing it away from his girl-friend.

The wolf moved in tandem to its attacker. Its eyes remained focused on the eyes of the boy. Its teeth were bared. It was ready. Ready for any opening. An opening that would allow it to spring at the boy, to dodge his weapon, and to sink its teeth into the fleshy neck of its tormentor.

The wolf had had a taste of blood from the horse. It wanted more. Ancient and primordial images flashed through its mind — images of running in a pack with other wolves, of a chase, of capturing a buffalo. Patience was the wolf's greatest weapon. And as in those days of old, it could wait — wait until this puny boy grew weary from swinging his weapon. Already, it could smell exhaustion coming from him.

Don's arms were numb. He swung the belt again and again. He had to get the wolf away from Gayle. He had to save his girlfriend. The only way to do so was to kill the giant wolf.

"DON!" Gayle called from behind him.

Don turned slightly, just for a split second. But it was enough time for the wolf to vault at him.

Don felt as though someone had slugged him with a steel pole. The wolf had thrown its entire body at him and caught him square in the chest.

He flew several feet back and hit the ground with such force that the air was again knocked out of him.

Now the wolf was on top of him, its eyes boring into his own. Its muzzle opened, slowly revealing the large teeth, and the hot, putrid breath of the beast beat down upon him.

Don grabbed the buckle and swung up, aiming the edge of the silver buckle for the wolf's neck.

"NO!" he heard Gayle scream. She sounded very far away.

Then he felt the sharp teeth of the wolf on his throat —

Darkness and eternity became one.

It was like a wave crashing down on him. An explosion smashed against his eardrums. The sound receded like churning waves escaping the shore. Don heard an ancient voice, thick with a foreign accent and heavy with pity.

> *"The way you walked was thorny —*
> *Through no fault of your own.*
> *But as the rain enters the soil,*
> *The rivers enter the sea,*
> *So tears run to a predestined end.*
> *Your suffering is over.*
> *Now you will find peace for eternity."*

The midway was only one hundred yards away. Don raised a hand toward the whirl of neon green, yellow, blue, and red lights. He could smell the dirt, the grease, the sweat, the deep-fried food.

No one on the midway had heard their screams of terror. Nor did anyone hear the howl of the giant wolf as it stood victorious over its victims. All was lost in the noise of people shouting, screaming, laughing, and the metallic grinding of gears and the numbing heavy metal music.

Don Earl drowned in the pitch-black flood of endless time.

CHAPTER ONE
Tuesday, Four Weeks Later
Ponce de Leon High School Cafeteria

Oh, brother! Nina Nobriega thought. *Here comes trouble. Double trouble!* She took a deep breath. Robert Hardin and Joe Motley were walking toward her.

Nina shook her head and returned to the long, thin balloons sitting before her. They were red, green, yellow, orange, white, purple, blue, and a weird shade of brown. These weren't just any balloons — they were the kind clowns tie together to make animals and hearts at little kids' birthday parties.

Nina's chemistry teacher, Mr. Cravens, had gotten the bright idea that his students could learn better if they were having fun. But fun to a teacher and fun to a student are as different as bologna and sirloin steak.

Each student chose a chemical model selected by lottery, literally from Mr. Cravens's Florida State baseball cap. Then the student had to build the model they'd selected. Not using pipe cleaners and painted Styrofoam balls, like a normal teacher would assign. Oh, no. Mr. Cravens wanted his students to use balloons.

As fate would have it, Nina had drawn the chemical model for bucky balls — or, known by its technical name, *Buckminster fullerenes*, a carbon model named after the physicist Buckminster Fuller. Nina's model called for football-shaped molecules that consisted of sixty carbon atoms made up of pentagons and hexagons — the toughest model to create.

So, here she sat in the cafeteria of Ponce de Leon High School with a thirty-gallon plastic garbage bag filled with sixty balloons. She had spent most of the previous night blowing them up.

And now Joe and Captain Bob were approaching her. Bob's cheeks were puffed out in a wide grin. Nina felt like a canary in a cage with a hungry cat approaching.

"Whatcha doing?" Bob asked, sitting down across from her. He tilted his faded black and well-worn captain's hat back on his head.

"Homework," Nina replied, without looking up. She was trying to tie two balloons at right angles.

"Here, I'll help." Bob grabbed several balloons and began tying them together.

"I don't want your help!" Nina protested. But it was too late.

In a matter of moments, Bob had tied several together in a tangled mass of reds and blues and greens and yellows.

"There!" he announced proudly, holding forth what he'd created. "A perfect model of the human intestines!"

Nina grabbed the mass of knotted balloons. "Just great." She began pulling at the balloons, trying to untie them. "I have just enough to do this project, and you've ruined it."

Bob reached toward the knotted balloons. "Here, I'll untie them," he said.

Nina pulled back. "No. You've helped enough. Just what do you two want, anyway?"

"Never mind him," Joe said. "Listen, we're having an emergency meeting of the Forensic Club this afternoon, and we'd like you to be there." Forensics was the study of applying scientific knowledge to examine evidence. The Forensic Club was devoted to studying crimes. Joe and Bob were members, along with Detective Turner, from the San Tomas Inlet police force, who was the club's advisor.

"Why?" Nina said. *I'd like to tie* his *intestines in a knot*, she thought as she continued to untangle the balloons.

"We're gonna induct a new member," Bob said.

"Really? Who?"

"You," Bob replied.

Nina didn't look up. "Why me?"

"Well, you did a good job helping to get rid of Count Dracula," Joe said. "We talked to Detective Turner, and he says we can add anybody we like."

"Besides," Bob added, "we need the dues."

Nina looked at Bob and then Joe. "Oh, really. And how much are the dues?"

"Twenty bucks," Bob said quickly.

Joe punched Bob in the arm.

"Hey!" Bob said, rubbing his arm.

"Five dollars," Joe said.

"You know," Nina began, "I'm photo editor of the yearbook and I don't remember ever getting a request to photograph any of your club's meetings or officers."

"We're an off-campus club," Bob said. "Mr. Haught wouldn't let us have the club on campus because we deal with *murder*." Bob growled, raised his hands, and made a halfhearted lunge for Nina.

Nina slapped his hands away.

"Owww! What am I today, the designated punching bag?" Bob protested.

"The fact that Mr. Haught doesn't allow you to have your club on campus is just an indication of how intelligent our principal actually is," Nina said, ignoring Bob's protest and returning her attention to the knotted balloons. "Just how many people have you got in this club?"

Joe cleared his throat. "Just two — for now. Me and Captain Bob."

"Really?" Nina asked with a raised eyebrow.

"Yeah," Bob chimed in. "Joe's president and I'm vice president as well as secretary."

"I've seen how you keep notes in class, Bob," Nina said. "I'd hate to see the minutes of your meetings."

"Minutes?" Bob said, puzzled. "We're supposed to keep minutes?"

Nina shook her head. *Freshmen,* she muttered. "So, with the two of you in the club, that means you have about ten bucks in your account."

"Actually —" Bob dug into his pockets, pulling out several coins. "We've got" — his head bobbed as he counted the coins — "thirty-five cents and one Russian ruble."

"Thirty-five cents?"

"Yeah," Joe said with a sigh. "Captain Bob's the treasurer, also."

"I figured as much." Nina smiled wryly. She looked at Captain Bob. "What are you doing with a Russian ruble?"

"My uncle sent it to me," he replied, holding up the small silver coin. "From Russia. He was transferred there last year to help set up a marketing firm. That's how I got this." Bob lifted the black, well-worn yacht captain's hat from his head.

"So, we have your uncle to blame for giving you that ratty-looking, smelly old hat?" Nina asked, grinning.

"Hey!" Bob pulled the yacht hat back on his head. "You dis the hat, you dis me!"

"I wish both of you would *dis*appear," Nina retorted.

"We're meeting at three-thirty," Joe said. "At the police station. Detective Turner's office."

"I'll try to make it," Nina said. "Right now, the most important thing in my life is trying to make a bucky ball from these balloons."

"A bucky ball?" Bob said. "Why didn't you say so? I thought you were just fooling around." Bob grabbed several balloons.

"Hey!" Nina shouted.

Too late. Captain Bob was already tying the balloons together.

"Ta-da!" he announced a few moments later. "One element of a bucky ball."

Nina's eyes widened. The freshman had indeed tied the balloons into a segment of a bucky ball. Nina gently took the segment from Bob.

"I'm impressed," she said. Instantly she was so startled that she had paid Bob a compliment that she almost choked.

"Thanks," Bob said. "I could do it blindfolded. Want to see?" He made a grab for more balloons.

Nina quickly put her hand against Bob's chest and gently pushed him back. "Uh, no thanks. I think I can handle it from this point."

"C'mon, Bob," Joe said as he stood. "We're going to be late for botany."

"Okay, buddy." Bob stood. Nina was examining the intricate knotting Bob had used. "Kinda makes you want to treat me with a little more respect, doesn't it?" Bob stood up straight, his chin held up, his chest puffed out.

Nina smiled. "Oh, I'm impressed, bucky ball boy. But, then again, I'm not really all that surprised that you're an expert with clown balloons."

Bob smiled. Then he frowned as he grasped the true meaning behind Nina's comment.

"C'mon, bucky ball Bob," Joe said with a laugh as he pulled his friend away from the table.

"I'm off, said the mad man!" Bob said with a deep, menacing, mad-scientist laugh.

Nina rolled her eyes. Bob never could resist that cheesy exit line.

3:45 That Afternoon
San Tomas Inlet Police Department

"Look, I admit that that business with the vampires was rather, shall we say, unusual," Detective Mike Turner was saying. "But I still say it was all a big gag, maybe by one of those shows that pulls practical jokes on people and then makes them look like idiots on television."

Bob had wanted to say, "I don't think you need a television show to make you look like an idiot." But he didn't. He respected Detective Turner, even when the older man was being stubborn.

Instead, Bob said, "If that's true, then why

haven't we heard anything about it, or been approached by a producer to get our permission to air what they filmed?"

"Maybe what they filmed wasn't good enough for their show." Detective Turner took a sip of coffee and grimaced. "*Yeech*. I hate cold coffee."

Joe shifted in his chair. "If this was a hoax, then it was the biggest hoax I've ever heard of."

Detective Turner leaned back in his chair and propped his feet on his desk. "I admit that there are still some unanswered questions. But let's look at what we have: All your friends turned out to be alive and well, and no one had any lasting injuries. Now, if they had been attacked by Dracula or Dr. Dunn or *any* vampire, there would be scars. Show me one scar, and I'll believe you."

Bob and Joe looked at each other. They couldn't produce one shred of evidence that Count Dracula had actually stepped out of the classic horror movie *Dracula* and into San Tomas Inlet, then proceeded to tear the town apart.

Even to Joe, the logic of the situation was, well, illogical. Sometimes, late at night, just before he fell asleep, he wondered if perhaps he hadn't dreamed of "borrowing" the defective three-dimensional projector from Universal Studios, or that Dracula had escaped from his movie during a freak electrical storm and tried to turn Nina's friend Angela into his vampire bride.

But Joe's logical mind told him that all of that

had happened. Captain Bob and Nina remembered it. Their friends remembered it. Even Detective Turner remembered looking for a vampire cult in the San Tomas Inlet area.

What made it nearly impossible to accept the truth was that all the evidence was either transported back into the original Universal Studios' 1931 version of *Dracula* or simply disappeared, as though it had never happened or existed. Like a movie: Once it's over, it's over. Except for the memories.

The final scenes of the battle with Dracula raced through Joe's memory. He had pointed the modified digital camcorder at the vampire, the monster had been vacuumed back into his fictional world — and so was all the evidence. Fade to black. The End. Just like the movies.

Except it wasn't all over yet. Five other monsters had escaped from their celluloid world the night they'd borrowed the projector. Now it looked like another one had struck.

Which was why they had called a meeting of the Forensic Club.

"Look, Detective Turner," Bob was saying, "none of us has a logical explanation for this, but we know it happened. We just want to know if you'll help us the next time we have to fight a monster."

Detective Turner laughed. "You know, I really like you boys. You're smart and you've got imagination. Just what a good detective needs. But" — he swung his feet from his desk and stood up — "a good detective also needs to know how to separate fact from fiction. And when he's being played for a fool." He took his revolver from a drawer and put it in his hip holster. "Now, if there's no further club business, I've got a date with some leftover meat-loaf, a stale bag of potato chips, a diet Coke, and an easy chair." He opened the door to his office.

"Well," Joe began, "we were expecting Nina to show up. To join the club."

"Maybe next time," Detective Turner said. He looked at his watch. "My shift's over."

Joe and Bob stood and walked out the door. Soon they were outside the small police station, skate-boards in hand.

"Why didn't you let me tell him about what I found on the Internet last night?" Bob asked.

"He still doesn't believe we fought and defeated Count Dracula," Joe said as they headed up the street, away from the police station. "You think he's gonna believe what you found?"

"Sorry I'm late, guys," Nina said, walking quickly up to the boys. "I had to finish that bucky ball and hand it in after school. Did I miss the grand initiation?"

"No," Bob said disconsolate. He raised his hands and wiggled his fingers like a bad magician. "There, you are now initiated into the Forensic Club." His voice was stern and flat, his light brown eyes fixed on hers.

Nina's smile faded. This wasn't like Bob. Captain Bob could find something witty to say while a building burned down around him.

She had known the two boys for nearly six months. All three had first met working as interns at Universal Studios Florida's theme park. They'd quickly become fast friends, as they shared a common interest in computers and classic horror movies.

Nina and Joe had gotten along well from the beginning. With his height — he stood at 6'1" in his stocking feet — and dark, serious look, Joe was often mistaken for a high-school senior. Nina still was amazed that he was only fourteen years old. What she liked most about him was that Joe was a gentleman in a generation of rude and crude teenage boys.

Captain Bob was another story. He could be leader of the rude and crude set. Nina and Bob had their differences. She didn't particularly like freshmen who acted like freshmen; he didn't particularly like people who didn't like freshmen. She didn't like his know-it-all attitude; he didn't like the idea that a *girl* was as smart as he was. He thought she was stuck-up. She thought he was gross. They each tried to outdo the other with quick, curt remarks that amounted to little more than verbal pepper spray.

However, they had one thing in common despite all of their differences: respect for each other. Nina had to admit (if only to herself) that despite Bob's childish antics and overactive imagination, he was fun to be around and she hadn't had a boring moment since they'd met. Besides, Bob was no coward. He could be counted on to help no matter how dangerous the situation became. He had proved that in their battle with Dracula.

"What's up?" she said, trying to hide the seriousness with which she asked the question.

"We've got a conflict," Bob responded. "Detective Turner thinks that our battle with Dracula was some sort of joke. We can't produce any evidence that the *real* Dracula actually escaped from his movie and then attacked us."

"So, what's the conflict?" Nina said.

"We just asked him if he would help us with the next monster," Bob replied.

"And?"

"And he laughed at us." Bob dropped his skateboard to the ground, placed one foot on the deck and pushed off with the other foot, moving slowly away from his two friends.

Bob could take any insult someone wanted to hurl at him, often replying with a quip that put the offender in his place. He didn't like violence, but he would stand his ground against a bully or a monster. He could even tolerate a little kidding about his short, stocky build, his uncontrollable dishwater-blond hair, or his beloved yacht captain's hat.

However, to be laughed at, not to be taken seriously, to be dismissed like some pesky child, gnawed at him.

Joe watched his friend glide down the sidewalk. "He's pretty conflicted."

"One thing you can say about Captain Bob," Nina replied with a sly smile, "he's got the courage of his conflictions."

Joe rolled his eyes. "Oh, *brother*! I think he's rubbing off on you."

"Man, I hope not. I don't think I could find a strong enough industrial soap to scrub him off."

Joe laughed.

"So, what's up?" Nina asked again.

Joe sighed. "Captain Bob called me last night at two in the morning."

"Doesn't surprise me," Nina said, smiling. "That boy has no sense of —"

"No, wait." Joe watched as Bob continued to move slowly away. Then he looked back at Nina. "The second monster has appeared."

Nina's smile quickly faded. Joe handed her the printout Bob had given him earlier that day.

Nina scanned it, her eyes widening as she read of cattle mutilations and the killing of cats and dogs. She shuffled to the second page, a newspaper report about a high school senior who was being held for the attempted murder of a carnival barker. The article noted that the high-school senior was a star on the Wales High School rodeo team and had been predicted to be national bulldogging champion. The article went on to quote the distraught teen as saying that he hadn't attacked anybody, that he was only defending his girlfriend and himself from a wolf — a giant wolf. A wolf that had stood on its hind legs like a man.

Nina looked up quickly at Joe. "It's *him*, isn't it?"

"Yep," Joe said, "the Wolf Man is killing cattle and people in Volusia County."

CHAPTER TWO
Friday Afternoon, 3:30 P.M.

"Have you packed the presses?" Dr. James asked.

"They're in the trunk," Captain Bob replied. "All three of them."

"Good. And you've got plenty of newspapers?"

"Yes," Joe said. He held a two-foot stack of old newspapers. "I think we've got enough to press every plant in the state of Florida."

"Good," Dr. James said with a laugh. "Now remember: I don't want anything to happen to the cabin. You're welcome to use anything in it, but if I find out you three have trashed the place, you two," he indicated Joe and Bob, "will be repeating this class next summer while your friends are enjoying their summer vacation." He looked at Nina. "You're in charge. You understand?"

Nina grimaced. She would rather baby-sit a bunch of gorillas.

"Gotcha," Captain Bob said with a salute.

"You got plenty of gas?" Dr. James said.

"Yes," Nina replied. "Oh, here are the permission

forms." She opened her notebook keeper and handed the teacher three sheets of paper.

Nina watched as Dr. James reviewed them. Dr. Thomas James was a little taller than her. He had thick dark black hair combed straight back, a prominent widow's peak revealing a hairline slowly creeping its way toward baldness. His bright copper eyes moved across the forms with speed and determination. His thin lips were pressed firmly together.

"Good. All signed, sealed, and delivered," he said. "I've called each of your parents and have given them the number to the cabin in case of emergency."

"I've also got my cell phone," Nina said.

"Good. Make sure to call your folks when you get there."

"Will do," Bob said as he hopped into the front seat of Nina's white Camaro convertible.

"I called shotgun," Joe said. He grabbed Bob by the shoulder.

"Ouch!" Bob said. "All right, already." Bob jumped from the front seat to the back.

"Hey! You'll be cleaning those seats with your tongue if you get your grimy feet on them!" Nina protested.

Dr. James shook his head and smiled. "I appreciate you taking these two to help with their plant collection, Nina," he said. "But I think you're a little crazy, too." He looked at the boys. "Now, guys,

Nina was the best botany student I had last term. She knows what you're looking for. She's surveyed the area before and can show you how to key the plants. Listen to her: your grade depends on it."

"Sure, Dr. James," Joe said.

"Will do, *mon capitan*," Bob said in bad French. He gave a twisted salute.

"Are you sure about this, Nina?" Concern showed on Dr. James's face.

Nina sighed. "Yeah. I guess." She fired up the engine.

"Well, good luck," he said, waving.

"I'm gonna need it," she said with a laugh as they drove away.

"Whew," Bob said as they exited the San Tomas Inlet high school parking lot and turned onto Beach Front Road. "I didn't think we'd ever get away from him. Talk about being a mother hen."

"Dr. James is one of the best teachers we have," Nina said. "You should be grateful he's letting you do this extra-credit project so you don't fail."

"*I'm* not failing," Joe said.

"I mess up on one lousy little test and my grade drops into the black hole of no return," Bob said. He folded his arms against the slightly chilly afternoon wind that whipped into the convertible's passenger seat.

"For someone with an IQ of 130, you seem to have a lot of trouble keeping your grades up," Nina said.

"My classes are boring," Bob replied. "I can't take any advanced classes until I'm a sophomore. Being a freshman is the pits."

"Most pits are freshmen," Nina said with mock seriousness. She glanced at Joe and winked. "Front seat company excluded, of course."

Joe smiled.

"Well, *this* is gonna be a fun trip," Bob yelled from the back, his voice cracking as he swallowed a rush of air.

"What did you tell your parents?" Nina said to Joe.

"I told them the truth. No sense in lying."

"What whopper did you tell your mom?" she asked Bob.

"Well, thanks to Mr. Integrity up there, I had to tell the truth, too. His mom called my mom before I could think of anything to tell her. She was already upset that I've got a D in Hepner's civics class, and now she knows that I'm on the verge of failing botany as well. I'm grounded for two weeks when we get back. I have to work at the Beach Burger on the weekends, plus I have to clean my room on a regular basis."

Nina and Joe suppressed the urge to laugh. What Captain Bob possessed in intelligence, he lacked in common sense. Ask him what the chemical signature for hydrogen peroxide was and he'd spit out H_2O_2 before you finished your question. Ask him what homework he had due the next day and he'd look at you with the blank face of a statue.

Nina turned the car onto Interstate 95 and they headed north.

They had a simple plan. Bob's near-failing grade in botany gave them the opportunity to investigate the sighting of a giant wolf in Wales, a small town north of Orlando and about sixty miles from San Tomas Inlet.

Wales was a rural town that straddled state highway 40. Most people would have never heard of Wales if not for the annual Rodeo and Founders' Day Festival and Carnival, which drew the best from among the state's high school rodeo competitors. The small rural town also acted as the eastern entrance into the Ocala National Forest.

Wales's strong agriculture base and large cattle ranches were out of place with the image most people have of Florida — sunny beaches, racing at Daytona, alligators in swamps, and enormous theme parks. The farming community of Wales looked as though it belonged more in Oklahoma or Texas than in the sunny vacationland known as Florida.

Bob asked, "Did you bring the camera?"

"Yes," Nina replied, looking at Bob in the rearview mirror. Bob nodded a little, pulled his leather jacket around him, and closed his eyes. She glanced to her side. Joe's eyes were closed, also.

Good. At least I'll have a little peace and quiet before we fight a werewolf.

Nina flipped open her CD case and pulled out a silver disk. She shoved it into her CD player.

John Fogerty's gravel-tinged voice darkly crooned, *"I see the bad moon arising."* Nina smiled a little ironic smile as the wind whipped through her shoulder-length brown hair.

Of the three, Nina had been the last to be convinced that the world's greatest vampire, Count Dracula, had been transformed from a specially digitized video image into a flesh-and-blood ghoul that preyed on the otherwise quiet city of San Tomas Inlet. She laughed to herself. And a dentist on top of that!

What she had found hardest to believe was that all of the classic Universal Studios monsters had disappeared from the special DVDs Bob and Joe had created to be used with the experimental three-dimensional projector they had merely intended to *borrow* from Universal Studios Florida's Research and Development Department.

Bob had been the first to jump at the idea of fighting the classic monsters. Of course, Bob jumped at anything that provided an excuse for him not to do his homework. If Bob was good at anything, he was good at creative avoidance. Joe had followed Bob's lead, but was more cautious.

Only after her best friend, Angela Chavarria, had been attacked was Nina convinced that, yes, indeed, they had unleashed the once mythological monsters of humanity's deepest and darkest fears onto an unsuspecting world.

And it was Nina who had fused the trio into a tight team of terror-fighters that had found and defeated the Dark Lord of the Night and sent the bloodthirsty Dracula back into his own world.

After Dracula was defeated, the trio had decided to search the newspapers and the Internet for any reports of strange and abnormal events. No one knew which monster would appear next.

Nina wasn't yet convinced the Wolf Man had made his deadly presence known. Wild dogs and cougars attacking pets and farm animals wasn't that unusual in rural Florida. However, unlike the first time, she wasn't going to dismiss the possibility that the second of the six deadly monsters was terrorizing a small Florida town without fully investigating the reports. Bob's favorite website had run several stories about the sightings.

She mentally reviewed the information Bob had been able to download. Most people interviewed by the papers believed that the teenager, a senior by the name of Don Earl Abernathy, might have indeed been attacked by a wolf. A horse belonging to Gayle Braddock, Don's girlfriend, had been killed. The police speculated that during the attack, a carnival barker by the name of John Winokea had come to help Don. The teenager, dazed, disoriented, and weakened by the loss of blood, had mistaken the man for the wolf and struck him in the side of the head with the edge of a large silver belt buckle. The force of the blow and the weight of the buckle were such that Winokea's skull was nearly crushed and the Native American was now in a coma at the Wales Community Hospital.

Don was in custody in the Wales city jail. However, because the attack took place on the Ocala Indian Reservation, the Ocala tribal police were claiming jurisdiction and wanted the teenager transferred to tribal authority where, as one angry Ocala elder put it, "We'll see that justice is done."

The normally peaceful and profitable relationship between the town of Wales and the Ocala Elder Council was strained. Many in Wales didn't want Don handed over to the tribal police and courts because they felt that judgment had already been passed on the young man. The Florida Bureau of Investigation and the Florida State Bureau of Indian Affairs were also involved in the dispute.

For now, Don Earl spent long days and even longer nights in the single small eight-by-ten-foot jail. A tutor from the high school brought him his daily homework.

Because of his arrest and impending trial, the high school rodeo hero had lost out on competing at the National High School Championship Rodeo and also lost his chance at a full four-year rodeo scholarship to Oklahoma State University.

Perhaps the cattle mutilations were just as the

traditional papers had reported them, Nina thought: attacks from cougars. At least that was the official line from the authorities.

Bob had not only downloaded the *official story* from newspapers and authorities but also the *real story* from several of the thousands of websites that spread reports about the strange and the weird. These sites had contradicted the police reports — they were to journalism what Spam was to meat.

According to the website, residents had reported the sightings of a giant wolf prowling the tree line of the Ocala National Forest and lurking in the vast cattle ranges. Some said that the wolf sometimes walked on its hind legs like a man and stood at least seven feet tall.

The site even devoted a whole cyber issue to *lycanthropy*, with exclusive quotes from Don Earl Abernathy:

Q: What did you see exactly?
A: A wolf. A giant wolf.
Q: What did it look like?
A: Like a giant wolf!
Q: What did it do?
A: It tried to kill us. It had already killed my girlfriend's horse. I was able to distract the wolf, and it attacked me.
Q: Did it bite you?
A: Yes, at the base of my neck on the left side.
Q: Why do you think it tried to kill you?

A: I don't know.

Q: What else happened?

A: It stood on its hind legs. Not like a trained dog. Like a man.

Q: What did it do when it stood on two legs?

A: I don't know. I passed out.

Q: Was it a werewolf?

A: A what?

Q: Werewolf. *An old German word:* were *means* man, *and* wolf *means —*

A: I know what a wolf IS! *And I know what a man* IS! *I don't believe in fairy tales!*

The interview ended.

None of that information was in the official newspaper accounts. Nina wasn't sure how reliable Bob's Internet connections were, but Joe was convinced that they had enough evidence to at least check it out. At times, Joe could be just as immature and prankish as Bob, but he wasn't rash, nor was he quick to embrace trouble.

Bob, on the other hand, would dash headfirst into trouble and want to go back for second helpings. Only afterward would he ask the important questions like *Who? What? When? Where?* and *How?* Lemmings often came to mind when she thought about Captain Bob and trouble.

Nina smiled to herself. She glanced up at the rearview mirror. Bob was sprawled out across the backseat, a small sliver of drool oozing out of the corner of his mouth. Nina laughed out loud.

Bob snorted and bolted to a sitting position.

"We there yet?" Bob said, a childlike dazed look on his face. Then he yawned and stretched. He tapped Joe on the back of the head. "Hey, Sleeping Beauty."

"I've been awake for the last fifteen miles," Joe said, stretching.

"We're just arriving," Nina said. "Dr. James said the cabin was right outside the forest, on the west side of town."

They drove down the center street of Wales. Large, super chain department stores had yet to reach the small community, so Wales still had a thriving downtown business — mostly mom-and-pop stores, some of which were just closing up for the day.

"*Yeech*," Bob said. "Did we transport back in time? I bet this place doesn't even have an Atomic Drive-in."

"What kind of word is that?" Joe said.

"What?"

"*Yeech*."

"It's a word?" Bob said. "I thought it was just a noise."

"I hope this cabin isn't as primitive as Dr. James said it was," Nina said as they drove out of the small town.

"I hope by primitive he meant that we can only get fifty cable stations instead of five hundred," Bob chimed in.

"I'd just be glad if it's got indoor plumbing," Joe said.

"Yeech," Bob said. "I hadn't thought about that."

"Hey!" Joe said suddenly.

"What?" Bob said leaning forward.

"There's an Atomic Drive-in!"

"Hallelujah!" Bob replied. "Civilization has reached the boondocks!"

"How about getting something to eat before we go to the cabin?" Joe asked Nina.

"Sure," she replied, flipping up her turn signal lever. "Could be the last decent meal we have for a while. No telling what's at the cabin."

"I brought some food," Bob said, holding up a brown grocery bag.

Nina glanced in the rearview mirror. "I don't even want to know." She guided the car into a slot and turned off the engine.

A short while later they were munching on Atomic burgers and greasy french fries while slurping on Meltdown milk shakes.

"'o," Bob mumbled as he shoved several fries into his already full mouth. "Whadaya 'ink? W' gon' ge' a were-wul?"

Nina scowled at Bob in the rearview mirror. "Yeah, we're just going to sic you on the Wolf Man with your mouth full. Once he sees your terrible manners, he's going to want to return to the more civilized world of his movie!"

Joe laughed and then snorted, freezing milk shake shooting into his nasal passages. "Ow, ow, ow! Brain freeze! Brain freeze!"

"Put your head between your knees," Bob ordered.

"That's for fainting," Nina corrected.

"Then put a bag over your head!"

"Just leave him alone," Nina said. "You okay?" she asked.

"Feels like the iceberg that sank the *Titanic* just collided with my brain."

"'U'll 'ive," Bob assured his friend, his mouth already full of food once again.

Nina started to laugh but stopped as a hand gripped her shoulder.

She turned and craned her neck upward. A big man loomed by the side of her car. The man was tall, even taller than Joe. He wore black jeans, a short-sleeved khaki shirt, and a tan cowboy hat. Patches on both sides of his shirtsleeves and the gold-plated star on the left side of his shirt said WALES POLICE DEPARTMENT. The plastic name tag on the right side of the shirt read SHERIFF MARSHALL. A large potbelly hung over his belt like a sack of flour.

"Ya kids ain't from 'round here, are ya?" His accent was of the old South, resonating on each syllable.

"Uh, no," Nina said, her heart still pounding. She

felt herself choke on a small piece of hamburger. She coughed.

The tall man frowned. "What are y'all doing in Wales?"

Nina cleared her throat. "We're —" she began, but her voice cracked. She cleared her throat again.

"We're staying at the old biological station by the Ocala forest," Joe volunteered.

"Ye-ah," Bob said, parroting a poor drawn-out southern drawl. "We's gonna be pickin' us'n's sum flow-ers."

The sheriff's eyes blazed at Bob. Bob swallowed hard.

"I'm Sheriff Marshall —" he began.

"Sheriff Marshall?" Bob said with a laugh. "Isn't that a bit redundant?"

The sheriff shot another dirty look at Bob. Bob remained quiet.

Nina had finally cleared her throat. She looked up at the sheriff. "We're from San Tomas Inlet," she began. "Our botany teacher, Dr. James, wants us to survey the plants in some of the sectors of the Ocala National Forest for a class project. We're staying at the old Central Florida University Biological Station."

"How long?"

Nina smiled, hoping that the sheriff didn't see the doubt behind the smile. "Through Sunday?"

"Y'all got anythin' to prove ya got permission?"

"Sure," Nina said. She turned to Joe and nodded

toward the glove compartment. Joe pulled out the letter Dr. James had written on Ponce de Leon High School stationery. "Here, sir."

The sheriff took the paper and unfolded it. He handed it back to Nina.

"Jest make sure y'all stay at the station and the sectors y'all are supposed to survey," he drawled. "Been some wild cougars about killing cattle and pets."

"Wild cougars?" Bob said. "Is there such a thing as tame cougars?"

The sheriff's eyes blazed again. Bob smiled what he hoped was a disarming smile.

"Yes, sir," Nina said.

"I'll have my deputy out to your place to check on ya," he said.

"Thanks," Nina said, but her voice trailed off as the sheriff turned and walked away, disappearing around the back of the Atomic Drive-in.

"Why do I suddenly hear banjos and someone shouting, *'Hee-Haw'*?" Bob said, a mocking frown on his face.

"I think," Joe began, "that we just time-warped back to the good ol' days. This place sure is different from the beach."

Nina started the car. She took the tray hanging off her slightly raised window and put it on the hooks at the speaker. She threw the car into reverse and quickly backed out.

"Hey!" Bob said as melted milk shake sloshed

out of his cup and onto his shirt. "This is my favorite shirt. It's been in my family for months."

"I just want to get to the cabin and unpack," Nina said. "Then we can check up on the werewolf story."

They had to exit around the back of the Atomic Drive-in to leave the parking lot. That's when Nina saw Sheriff Marshall sitting in a battered four-door sedan with peeling paint and rusty hubcaps. The interior of the car was dark, but Nina swears to this day that she saw two glowing red eyes shooting out at her like lasers, trying to penetrate her very soul.

CHAPTER THREE
An Hour Later, Wales Municipal Building

"Who are ya again?" the young man asked as he pushed thick-lensed, black horn-rimmed glasses up his greasy nose.

"I'm Joe Motley," Joe replied. "I'm from San Tomas Inlet."

"And what do ya want with Don Earl?"

"I just want to talk with him. I'm doing a report on teen violence for our school's newspaper." Joe swallowed. He was always uncomfortable when he told a lie, even if there was some truth to it. He did plan on writing a report about his meeting with Don Earl Abernathy, but not for the school newspaper. His report would be for the official Forensic Club journal.

"I'm sorry," the young man said. "Don Earl is under custody and only his lawyer and parents can see him."

"Oh," Joe said, trying to look as disappointed as possible. "Perhaps I could get a quote from you about teen violence in society." Joe pulled out a pencil from his shirt pocket and a reporter's notebook from his hip pocket.

A smile resembling a large crescent formed on the young man's face. "Yeah. Sure." He sat behind a large old wooden desk. He straightened up to a rigid sitting position. He wore the same black jeans, khaki shirt, and cowboy hat as Sheriff Marshall, the shirt decorated with the same arm patches and gold-plated badge. Except this badge said DEPUTY SHERIFF. And he didn't have a professionally engraved name tag on of his shirt as Sheriff Marshall had. Rather, he had one of those *Hello, My Name Is* name tags with blue borders. In the white center was scrawled *Deputy Barnes* with a felt pen so thick that the letters all ran together.

"Go ahead. What do ya want to know?" he asked with the same crescent smile.

"Well, first —"

The deputy stood with such suddenness that the old wooden chair grated against the wooden floor. Joe jumped back.

"Maybe I should stand, huh?" Deputy Barnes shouted. He pulled at his gun belt and tucked in his shirt.

"It really doesn't matter," Joe said. "I just want to ask you a couple of questions."

Deputy Barnes pulled his gun from its holster.

Joe jumped back farther, his eyes wide, his hands out in front of him.

"Maybe I ought to put a bullet in my gun, huh?"

Deputy Barnes leaned forward and looked around. Then he whispered so no one else could hear him, although he and Joe were the only ones there. "Sheriff Marshall don't like me to have bullets in my gun." He raised his eyebrows and smiled. "He thinks I can't be safe with bullets in my gun."

Joe's eyebrows raised. "Why?" he said, his voice raised slightly.

Deputy Barnes rolled his eyes again. "*Well*, you see, I was practicing my fast draw, ya know, like in the old Western days, and one time as I was drawing against Billy the Kid — just pretending like, ya know? — Sheriff Marshall comes walking in the door just as I drew. Well, he scared me so much that my gun accidentally went off." The young deputy chuckled. "Boy howdy, ya should have seen the look on Sheriff Marshall's face. You'd have thought the sweet chariot was a-swinging low just to personally take him home."

Suddenly, Joe wished he hadn't volunteered to try to interview Don Earl Abernathy. He swallowed hard and deep. "What h-happened?"

"*Well*, the bullet just flew over Sheriff Marshall's hat. No harm really."

"Do you think I can talk to Don?" Joe asked quickly.

Deputy Barnes's face went blank and then the crescent smile turned upside down. He holstered the gun. "Ya mean ya don't want ta talk to me any longer."

Joe pretended to write in the reporter's notebook. "I got it all down here," he said with a smile.

The deputy straightened and hitched his thumbs in his gun belt. "Who did ya say you are again?"

Joe cleared his throat. "I'm his brother."

The deputy looked Joe up and down.

"Don Earl doesn't have a brother."

"Uh . . . he's like a brother. We're both in the same school club."

"What club?"

"Oh, you know, your usual kind of high school club."

"You mean the Rodeo Club at Wales High School?"

"Yeah. That's it."

"Well, I guess it won't hurt. I know I'd hate to be in jail and not see any of my buddies." The deputy flicked a stubby thumb at the door behind the desk. "Go on in."

"Sure. Thank you, sir." Joe pushed the door open and went inside.

Joe was expecting a hallway lined with cells on either side. Instead, he walked into a small room, eight by ten feet, with a cot against one wall, a sink and toilet on the other, and a small desk and chair against a third wall. On top of the small desk was a tray of crusted-over food — a burnt and shriveled hot dog without a bun, some hardened yellow substance that once was potato salad, white bread that was so dry it was curling at the edges, and a half-pint carton of milk with a smiley face on the front.

A lone low-watt bulb washed the room with a dim light that cast a dingy haze over everything. There was a window above the desk, but it was small and grubby. Only the bravest and most persistent ray of sunlight could force its way through.

Don Earl Abernathy lay on the cot, an arm thrown across his eyes. He was dressed in a faded orange jumpsuit. Stenciled across the front in black were the words DOC — WALES. He wore faded and tattered blue slippers and no socks.

Joe walked softly to the edge of the bed. The low sound of breathing told Joe that Don was sleeping. Joe sighed. He had made it into the so-called jail cell only to discover that the inmate was asleep.

Joe was debating whether to awaken the teenager or return the next day. *I got in once; I can get in again.* He turned to go.

"Who are you?" The voice was weak, almost a whisper. "You're not a doctor. Are you a cop?"

Joe turned back toward Don and stood beside the bed.

"My name is Joe. I'm from San Tomas Inlet."

"What do you want?" Don Earl did not remove his arm from his eyes. "Who are you?"

"My name is Joe Motley. I'm a freshman in high school."

Don removed his arm from in front of his eyes.

He squinted. His intense, bloodshot eyes moved up and down. A chill snaked down Joe's body.

"High school? You look like you're big enough to be a freshman in college."

"Good genes, I guess."

Don's eyes lost their intensity. Then he smiled and coughed. "It only hurts when I laugh," Don said.

"Sorry," Joe said.

"No. It's okay. I've been poked and prodded and questioned by doctors and the police. It's nice to have someone who isn't so serious." Don swung his legs around and sat on the edge of the bed. "What do you want? How did you get in here?"

"Told the deputy we were brothers."

"I don't have a brother."

"That's what he said. So I told him we were in the same club at school."

"Are we in the same club at school?" Don smiled.

Joe returned the smile. "We don't even go to the same school." Joe shifted his weight.

"Excuse my bedside manner," Don said. "Have a seat."

"Thanks." Joe pulled a chair next to the bed.

"What do you want?" Don Earl repeated, his eyes never leaving the big freshman. "You some sort of volunteer? You know, the ones who visit prisoners and help them feel better about being caged up and all, or are you just some freak who likes talking to jailbirds?"

"Actually," Joe began, "I'm interested in getting

to know your tailor. I've always wanted a pair of orange overalls like those. You know, the right clothes could get me a date with the prom queen."

Don Earl smiled. He stood and walked over to the sink. He filled a plastic glass with water and drank quickly.

"What do you want?" he asked again as he sat the glass on the edge of the sink.

Joe decided not to stand. Don looked like he could handle himself. At over six feet, Joe was an imposing figure, even if he was only fourteen years old. He had learned long ago that people felt intimidated, threatened by his size.

Joe looked at the food. "You not hungry for the special of the day here? I can bring you something from the Atomic Drive-in."

"Forget it. But thanks. I don't eat meat."

"What?"

"I'm a vegetarian."

"I thought you were a cowboy?"

Don smiled. "You think because I'm a cowboy, I eat animal flesh?"

"Well, I never really thought about it."

"That's like saying all oversized high school freshmen are stupid."

Joe nodded. What was it Captain Bob was always saying? *Never speak in absolutes.* "Actually, I'm interested in giant wolves," Joe said flatly.

Don's eyes did not react. They continued to stare at Joe.

"The newspapers said you were attacked by a giant wolf."

"No. They didn't," Don said slowly. "They said I was attacked by a cougar and that I nearly beat a man to death."

Joe took a deep breath. "Okay. Uh, some sites on the Internet said you were attacked by a giant wolf."

"What sites?"

Joe shifted in his chair. "Uh, sites about paranormal and weird things."

"Oh," Don said.

"So? Were you attacked by a cougar or a giant wolf?"

"What do you think?"

"I think I'll listen to what you have to say, and then make up my mind."

"Who are you?"

"I'm someone who can help you — if you were attacked by a giant wolf."

Don raised his glass — then he sat it on the small dull chrome shelf above the sink. Joe noticed for the first time that there was no mirror above the sink.

Don walked past Joe and sat on the edge of the cot, his legs spread apart, his forearms resting on his legs, his head down.

"The papers were wrong. There hasn't been a cougar in Volusia County in twenty years. I was attacked by a giant wolf."

"Why did you attack the carnival barker?"

"I didn't attack anyone. I was trying to protect my girlfriend from the wolf. The wolf had just killed her horse and was going after her."

"But they found a man with a large gash and a cracked skull. You were found holding the belt buckle that caused it."

Don looked up at Joe without raising his head. His groan was quiet, almost inaudible. He took a couple of deep breaths and then said, "I didn't attack anybody. I was protecting Gayle."

"What do you remember after you struck the wolf with the edge of the belt buckle?"

"Nothing. Everything went black. I thought I was going to die. The wolf was trying to rip out my throat."

"Reports said that you claim you were bitten?"

"*Claim*?" Don grunted. "I *was* bitten. Here." Don pulled back the top of his orange jumpsuit to reveal the base of his neck. He pointed at the spot. "He bit me. Clean through to the bone. Blood was coming out of me like a geyser. That's when everything went black."

Joe looked at the skin. It was tan from years of working in the weather and the sun. But it was also smooth. If he had been bitten to the bone, he would have a scar like the Grand Canyon. But the skin was smooth and shiny.

"Yeah," Don Earl said, sensing Joe's doubts. "It ain't there. It was there at the hospital when they took me to the emergency room. Then the next morning it was gone, and that's when they brought me here." He fanned one arm around the room. "Hilton Hotel!"

"How big was the wolf?" Joe said.

"Ever see an Irish wolfhound?" Joe shook his head. "They stand six feet tall on their hind legs. The wolf that attacked me was bigger than an Irish wolfhound."

"Why do you think the wolf attacked your girlfriend?"

"I don't know."

Joe shrugged. "Maybe she knows," he said more to himself than to Don.

"What?" Don's eyes narrowed and stared at Joe.

Joe cleared his throat. "My friends are at your girlfriend's house trying to find out what happened."

Don stiffened. He glared at Joe, his eyes red with anger. "Tell them to leave her alone!" But his voice was deeper, almost a growl.

"What?" Joe said, startled. He sat up.

"She's mine!" Don said, his voice deep and rough.

"I'm sure they're only asking her a few questions. We've come here to help you."

Don stood — or, rather, he jerked up, his joints cracking and popping. His chest heaved as he breathed deeply.

Joe stood — slowly, so as not to alarm Don.

Don lowered his head and looked up at Joe. The rodeo star's deep brown eyes changed to a dull red. His voice quieter but still deep and rough. "It burnssss."

"What's wrong? Do you want me to call the deputy?"

A low, piercing growl echoed through the room. Joe jumped back, knocking the chair over.

Don straightened to his full height. His head snapped back as though slapped by some invisible force. His throat ballooned out to twice its size and a sound somewhere between a frog's croak and the growl of Cerebus the Hound of Hell reverberated against the four walls of the small room.

Don reached up with his hands toward the dull, low-watt bulb in the ceiling. He howled. He ripped the top of the orange jumpsuit. Joe gasped as he saw the bluish-red wounds that covered the left side of Don's neck and shoulder. Wounds that were deep and dotted about his flesh. Wounds that looked as though they were caused by the large, sharp teeth of a bear — or a giant wolf.

Ripples and bubbles appeared under Don's jumpsuit. He grew taller. Don screamed. His bones and joints and muscles and ligaments popped and cracked as his body stretched toward the ceiling. The orange jumpsuit ripped and tore to accommodate his expanding height and the muscles that swelled without mercy. His arms flailed above his head in a spasm of pain and horror. And then he connected with the lone light, striking and shatter-ing the dull, low-watt bulb.

The room went dark. A small square of haze ap-peared in the middle of the wall where the desk sat. Joe realized that the sun had set and evening had lowered its dark shadow on Wales, Florida.

"What's going on in there?" Deputy Barnes yelled as he rushed into the room, a burst of light following him. "Oh, my —" he began, but he didn't get a chance to finish.

Don swung out and backhanded him. The deputy flew across the room, slammed into a wall, and slumped to the floor, unconscious.

The door slowly closed, engulfing the room in the rusty dimness of evening.

Joe had backed up into the opposite corner of the room. A dark corner. The only light in the room came from the last few orange and brown sun rays of the dying day through the dingy window.

Joe's eyes adjusted to the dimness, and he watched as Don's body began to change, to grow even larger. The middle of Don's face extended out until the nose and mouth were now the snout of a dog. Hair burst from every pore of his skin — dark, thick hair that slithered out and covered every square inch of flesh.

Don's legs bent backward at the knee, the liga-ments and kneecaps snapping and cracking. Don fell to the floor onto his hands and what were now hind legs. His hands turned into fleshy balls that spurted forth the same coarse hair and long, black claws. His back arched. The jumpsuit ripped down the middle of his back. Don's spine rose at the center of his back and deep ridges formed where there should have been nobs of spinal cord.

A long, high-pitched howl pierced the evening silence. The window shattered. A bloodred moon had risen and was now framed in the broken window.

As quickly as it had begun, it was all over. And a funereal quiet filled the room.

Joe wasn't looking at Don Earl Abernathy anymore. He wasn't even looking at a human being. He was looking at something that existed in the half-light half-dark world between man and beast. A monster once found only in the deep, dark pit of primitive man's past.

Joe was staring at a werewolf.

The creature moved its head slowly from side to side. The transformation was complete. It smacked its lips and bared its teeth, revealing black gums and sharp teeth that gleamed wet in the moonlight.

Joe used every ounce of concentration and strength to keep himself from shivering from fear. Goosebumps crawled over his skin like a cold snake. He held his breath.

The werewolf walked to the deputy and sniffed at his face. Then it sniffed at the thick horn-rimmed glasses, which sat askance on the deputy's greasy nose. The werewolf snorted and looked around the room.

Joe remained still. His face felt hot. He hadn't taken a breath for what seemed like an eternity. A moment later, his body began to tingle, fighting against his will, telling him to breathe, to give his body the life-sustaining oxygen it needed. Joe knew he wouldn't last much longer. He only hoped that the werewolf would escape from the room before Joe either breathed deeply or fainted from lack of oxygen.

Joe finally gasped, gulping in air.

The werewolf's head snapped around. Then it turned its whole body and faced Joe. The monster's eyes were a bright, luminous red that seemed to shoot out from his pupils like lasers.

Joe took slow, silent breaths. If anything, he knew he would have to have the strength to fight the werewolf when it attacked. The werewolf moved slowly toward him. Joe tensed his muscles, ready for the monster to leap toward him. He bent his knees and raised his hands, which were balled into tight fists.

The monster moved to within two feet of Joe.

Then it stood on its hind legs. It grew larger as it stood. Joe knew he didn't have a chance. *The best defense is a good offense*. He lunged at the beast, butting his head into the werewolf's midsection. Joe and the werewolf flew across the cot and rolled to the opposite side.

Joe jumped up. The werewolf rose slowly and towered over him. It breathed heavily. In the reddish moonlight, Joe saw the werewolf open its mouth and curl back its lips. It growled. A soft growl. A growl of low tones and menacing meaning.

The werewolf swiped at Joe with the long, razor-like claws of his right paw. Joe ducked and then jumped up on the cot. At least now he was the same height as the werewolf. He stood face-to-face with the monster. The werewolf began to growl again —

Joe landed a right cross to its jaw. The werewolf staggered backward. Joe quickly planted a left jab on the tip of the werewolf's black nose. The werewolf fell back against the wall, howling in pain.

Then it lunged at Joe. Joe kicked out, trying to connect with the werewolf's rib cage, hoping to knock the wind out of it.

Instead, the werewolf grabbed Joe's leg. Joe hopped about the bed as he tried to free his leg from the powerful grasp of the monster. He felt himself losing his balance. Then, as he fell, he kicked out with his left foot, hitting the werewolf in the same soft spot his left jab had hit. The werewolf howled again and fell against the wall. Joe fell off the opposite side of the bed. He quickly jumped to his feet.

The werewolf lunged at Joe again, hitting him in the chest with the full weight of a seven-foot monster. Joe hit the wall and fell to the floor. His head swam between the light of consciousness and the darkness of deep sleep. He shook his head, trying to stay awake, but it only added to the painful pounding now hammering at his brain.

The monster now stood over Joe. It raised its right hand. The long, sharp claws glistened in the moonlight. Joe thought he saw a smile on the were-wolf's face.

A sudden burst of light and an explosion filled the room. It both blinded and deafened Joe. He fell to his side, screaming and holding his ears. His eyes squeezed shut against the red-and-white glare that had burned of the back on his eyeballs.

Through his own screams he heard the horrific cry of pain from the werewolf. Then he heard another scream — a high-pitched scream that rever-berated off the cold concrete walls of the jail cell. A human scream of sudden and terrible death. Next, there was the shattering of glass. And the room was quiet.

Joe opened his eyes, trying to get them to focus. He saw Deputy Barnes on the other side of the room, his smoking pistol still in his hand, his Buddy Holly glasses listing to the right. He looked lifeless.

At least he was able to load one bullet and shoot the werewolf with it.

Joe stood slowly and moved to the window. He stumbled as he reached the shattered window. He fell to his knees and looked out into the still night. He fought to remain conscious, drinking in the cool night air. A black swirling mass formed before his eyes and began to suck him into its whirlpool.

The last thing that Joe saw before he succumbed to the maelstrom was the full moon in the early evening sky. Silhouetted against the moon was a giant wolf standing on its hind legs, its head raised to the sky, a howl of horror and death pouring forth from its maw in tribute to the full bloodred moon that had given it birth.

CHAPTER FOUR
At the Same Time
But Not the Same Place

"You know," Captain Bob began, "I can't figure out why a smart teacher like Dr. James would leave teaching college to teach a bunch of high school kids. I mean, the guy's a *doctor*."

"I'm glad they could get him," Nina said. "He's the best science teacher I've ever had. I think it's cool that a college professor would want to teach high school kids. I actually like science now. His botany class last term was the best." She slowed the car. "Here we are."

"Yeech," Bob said.

Nina and Captain Bob pulled into a long driveway of one of the cattle ranches that dotted the western half of Volusia County. They passed under a sign that read BOUNCING B RANCH.

"Welcome to Hickville," Bob said.

"Be quiet, Bob," Nina admonished the freshman. "This is someone's home." She stopped the car in front of the house.

"Gee, talk about cliché," Bob said as he examined the modest but comfortable home before them. "A ranch home on a ranch."

"Bob, I'm warning you," Nina said through gritted teeth.

"Okay. Okay," Bob said, raising his hands in defense.

They got out of the car and walked up to the house. Nina rang the doorbell. Bob tilted his hat onto the back on his head.

Several long minutes later, the door opened. Opened just a crack, not enough to see who was standing on the other side.

"What do you want?" came a gruff female voice.

"That's no way to ans —" Bob began.

"We're looking for Gayle Braddock," Nina interrupted. She stepped in front of Bob.

"What do you want?"

"We heard about what happened and —" The door slammed shut in Nina's face.

Nina looked at Bob. He said, "I guess manners aren't at the top of the social do's and don'ts in Wales."

Nina rang the doorbell again.

"GO AWAY!" came a shout from within. "I'm not crazy. I'm not talking to any more reporters!"

"Gayle, we want to talk about what happened to you and your boyfriend." Nina waited. Silence hung in the air for several moments. "Gayle," Nina said softly but loud enough to be heard through the door. "*We* believe you."

Another long silence. Then the door slowly opened.

Gayle held the door open just wide enough to get a good look at the two teenagers standing on her front porch. One was a tall girl with straight, shoulder-length brown hair and brown eyes that had a small sparkle in each corner. She held herself erect and with confidence.

The other one was a boy not much taller than Gayle, and thick. He wore a black yacht cap with tufts of dirty-blond hair poking out beneath it as though they were trying to escape the head to which they were attached. His clothes were clean, but wrinkled. He wore a black leather jacket. He wasn't dirty or smelly or unattractive. What was the word she was trying to remember? One of a million vocabulary words her English teacher forced-fed the students each week.

Unkempt. That was it. He was cute, but unkempt.

"How can I help y'all?" Gayle said, trying to sound polite without being too inviting.

Bob Hardin felt a quiver in his stomach at the sound of the girl's voice. It was all sweetness and Dixie.

He took off his hat and held it down at his side. He smoothed down his hair. "Howdy do, ma'am?" he said in his best Rhett Butler.

Nina glanced at Bob with a frown and a roll of her eyes. "Hello. Gayle?" she said softly.

"Yes," Gayle answered.

Bob's stomach quivered again. He was about to speak but Nina cut him off.

"My name's Nina and this is —"

"Bob," Bob said, stepping in front of Nina. "Captain Bob. We're here to help you."

"What?" Gayle said. "What are you selling?"

Nina elbowed Bob behind her.

"May we come in, Gayle?" Nina said.

"I'm not supposed to let anyone in when my folks aren't home."

"We're harmless," Nina said with a smile. "Honest." She nodded toward Bob. "And he's house-trained, I promise."

Bob frowned and was about to whip out one of his cut-them-off-at-the-knees quips when he saw Gayle smile. He had to smile, too.

"My folks will be back just any minute now." Gayle didn't move.

Nina could tell Gayle was trying to make up her mind. "Would it help if we just talked out here on the porch?" she asked.

"I'd prefer it, if y'all don't mind," Gayle replied. "I don't want to be rude, but things have been just a little crazy the last month." She stepped outside.

The sun was slowly setting and long shadows cast their furtive forms across the lawn.

"We can sit out back by the pool," Gayle said. She shut the door. "This way, please."

Nina and Bob followed Gayle around the house

to a small patio that sat next to an oval-shaped pool. The sun's last rays danced and sparkled on the ripples of the bluish water.

"Please, have a seat." Gayle waved to lounge chairs on the patio.

"Thank you," Nina said.

"Yeah, thanks," Bob chimed in as he seated himself directly across from Gayle.

Gayle Braddock wore no makeup. She was dressed in oversized, frumpy gray sweats, and her blond hair was pulled into such a tight bun that it looked like it hurt. Her crystal-blue eyes were dulled by the red puffiness that encircled them.

Crying or sleeplessness or both, Bob thought. *No matter. She's still beautiful.*

"How can I help you?" Gayle said with genteel sincerity.

"No," Bob said with a wink, "how can *we* help *you*?"

"Oh, my *Aunt Bessie*!" Nina said with a groan. She turned to Gayle. "We've read about what happened at the carnival."

"Then you know that some people want to hang my boyfriend for attempted murder."

"Actually," Bob began, "the state of Florida gives a convicted murderer two options — *hey!*" Bob yelled at Nina. "That's my foot you stomped on."

Nina gritted her teeth. "It's gonna be your brain next time."

"Okay, okay. *Jeez.*" He turned to Gayle and smiled.

Nina sighed deeply. "We've read what the papers had to say and we've even read some of the stuff on the Internet. We've also read some of the police reports."

"How could you do that?" Gayle said. "I haven't even been able to see them. Sheriff Marshall's got them all locked up."

Bob raised his hand slightly from the table. "Uh, that's my doing. I've got a friend on the San Tomas Inlet police force, and he asked your sheriff for a copy of the files to help on a similar case."

"Where?"

"We're from San Tomas Inlet," Nina responded. "It's on the east coast, about forty miles from Orlando."

"Oh, yeah," Gayle said. "I've been swimming there."

"Ever eat at the Beach Burger?" Bob said, his eyes bouncing.

"No," Gayle replied, thinking. "I don't think so. Don's a vegetarian and we don't usually eat at fast-food places."

"Who?" Bob said, puzzled.

"Her boyfriend, Bob," Nina reminded him.

"Oh, yeah."

"Anyway," Nina said, turning back to Gayle. "We know what the newspapers and the Internet and the police have to say. We'd like to know what you have to say."

"You're not really grown-ups who look like kids

and are trying to get me to do an interview for one of those trashy talk shows, are ya?" Gayle asked.

"No," Nina said, smiling. "I'm a junior. Bob is a freshman."

"Yep," Bob chimed in.

"You're brother and sister?"

"What?" Nina said, startled. The thought of having Captain Bob Hardin as a 24/7 brother made her squirm. "No. We're just friends."

"But why do you want to know about what happened to Don Earl and me?"

"We belong to the Forensic Club," Bob said. "We're interested in solving crimes. Detective Mike Turner of the San Tomas Inlet police department is our sponsor."

"I see," Gayle said dully, though she really didn't understand.

"Can you tell us what happened?" Nina said.

"Pretty much what the papers reported," Gayle said. "Except that it wasn't any cougar that attacked us. It was a giant wolf. It killed Miss Prissy first."

"Who?" Bob said.

"My horse. I won the barrel racing championship with her, and then that beast killed her." She buried her face in her hands and sobbed.

Nina reached out and placed her hand softly on Gayle's forearm. "Are you sure it was a wolf?"

Gayle raised up. She wiped tears from eyes. "Yes. It came for me and Don Earl fought it off."

She sniffed. "But he didn't attack that man!" she burst out.

"What do you remember exactly?" Nina said.

She sniffed again. Her lower lip quivered. "We were running from the stables. The wolf hit both of us. It was a giant. I almost passed out after I hit the ground. I saw Don grab my belt and start whipping the wolf with it."

"Your belt?" Bob said.

"Yes. My trophy for being barrel racing champion. It had a buckle about this big." She held up her hands to form an oval shape about half the size of a professional football. "It was pure silver with a rider and a horse going around a barrel in gold."

"Pure evil can only be killed with pure silver," Bob said softly to Nina.

"Shh," Nina replied. "Did you see Don attack the carnival barker?"

"No. I must have passed out. When I came to, I was on a stretcher in the ambulance. I started screaming because Don wasn't there. Then they told me he was in another ambulance going to the hospital. Then I fainted again.

"The next morning when I woke up, my mom told me about the carnival barker, that Don had tried to kill him. I told her that Don was attacked by a giant wolf. She said that Don told the same story, but Sheriff Marshall wasn't believing either of us. And the Ocala tribal police wanted to arrest Don."

"Gayle!" someone called behind them.

They all jumped up from their seats. Nina and Bob turned around. A woman in her late thirties raced up to the three teenagers. She was Bob's height and looked like a more mature version of Gayle.

"I'm okay, Mom," Gayle said. "These are my friends."

"Honey, I was so worried when we saw that strange car and then couldn't find you in the house." Mother and daughter hugged.

"I'm okay," Gayle said again, reassuringly. "Where's Daddy?"

"Gayle, honey," Mrs. Braddock began, "your daddy's with Sheriff Marshall and Don's father."

"Don's father? Why?" A quiver shook the words from Gayle's mouth.

"Please, honey, I don't want you to get upset again. You haven't been able to sleep for the last month."

"My name is Nina Nobriega, Mrs. Braddock." Nina held out her hand and the older woman took it. "This is Bob Hardin. He's a friend, too."

"Ma'am," Bob said with a nod.

"Mom! Why is Daddy with Sheriff Marshall and Mr. Abernathy?" Gayle's voice cracked and tears welled in her eyes.

"Gayle, honey." Her mother's voice cracked and Nina could tell that she, too, was fighting back tears. "Don's escaped jail. He beat up Deputy Barnes and some other teenager and then jumped out the window. Your daddy and Mr. Abernathy are with Sheriff Marshall because they're afraid that if the sheriff finds Don Earl alone, he'll kill him!"

CHAPTER FIVE
Two Hours Later
Wales Memorial Hospital

Captain Bob looked down at his best friend. Joe was breathing deeply but quietly. His left cheek was swollen and his right eye was black. His Hawaiian shirt was torn and one of his shoes was missing.

Strange, Bob thought. *Who would want to steal one shoe? Especially a size seventeen extra wide!*

Joe moaned.

"I think he's coming around," Bob said to Nina.

"Good," Nina replied. She stepped closer to the bed. Joe opened his good eye.

"Hey, buddy," Bob said with a smile. "You were supposed to just talk to the guy, not tear his cell apart."

"Where . . . ?"

"Emergency room two," Nina answered. "Doctor said you don't have anything worse than a few bruises and a black eye."

"My head feels like a train hit it." Joe tried to sit up, but fell back against the bed.

"Not yet, buddy," Bob said. "Doc says you've got

to stay a little while longer. Just for observation. Although I don't know what there is to observe around here." Bob stepped to the side. An ancient and withered nurse was behind him, writing in a chart. Her support hose were rumpled at her ankles and her gray-streaked hair clung to her head like wire with static electricity. "This is Nurse Stonewall," Bob said. He leaned closer. "And I ain't making that name up, either!"

Joe smiled. "Oww. That hurt."

"Only when you smile, huh?" Bob said.

Joe looked at his friend. "Don said that earlier."

"What did Don Earl say?"

Joe turned his head slightly. There was a girl standing just behind Nina. She was pretty with blond hair and blue eyes.

"This is Gayle," Nina said. "Don's girlfriend."

Joe tried to raise his hand toward the girl but could not. It fell back to the bed with a thud.

"Feels like lead," he said.

"That's the sedative," Nurse Stonewall said. "It's wearing off. You were thrashing around so much, the doctor thought you would hurt yourself." She wrote on the chart and then looked at her watch. "The doctor says you can leave in another ten minutes. And not a minute sooner." She turned and marched from the room.

"Slime on rocks is more appealing," Bob said.

Joe smiled. "Oww. Oww. Oww. Got to remember not to smile for a while."

"What did Don say?" Gayle repeated.

Joe looked at the girl and then at his two friends.

"It's okay," Nina assured him. "She knows why we're here."

Joe's eyes darted around the room and his face twisted. "What about Deputy Barnes?"

Bob said, "Well, Deputy Barnes is in emergency room one. He's beaten up like you, but he's okay."

"He got off one shot," Nina added. "He must have hit what he was aiming for because there's a lot of blood by the window and outside on the grass."

"He saved my life," Joe said softly.

"Saved your life from who?" came a deep voice from behind them.

They all turned. Sheriff Marshall stood holding back the white curtain around Joe's bed.

"Hello, Sheriff Marshall," Gayle said.

"Gayle," the sheriff replied with a tip of his cowboy hat.

The man stepped into the room. He was taller even than Joe and towered over Bob.

"Doctor Leveritt called and said that Don Earl had attacked you" — he nodded toward Joe "— and tried to kill one of my deputies."

"That's not true!" Gayle shouted. "Don wouldn't hurt a fly."

The sheriff turned to Gayle. "We've been through this before, Gayle."

"Don is not a killer. He didn't attack that carnival worker and he didn't attack Deputy Barnes!"

"If he didn't," Sheriff Marshall began, "then who did? Your giant wolf?"

Tears welled in Gayle's eyes. She turned and ran from the room. Nina started after her.

"You stay here, little lady," the sheriff ordered. "I've got some questions for you three."

Nina shot the tall sheriff a look. "I'm not your *little lady*, and unless you want to arrest me, I'm going to help my friend." Nina flipped back her brown hair and left the room.

Sheriff Marshall watched her leave, then looked at Bob.

Bob smiled and shrugged his shoulders. "Hey, you just met her. Wait until you become one of her friends — then she really turns on the charm."

The sheriff frowned and turned back to Joe. "Want to tell me what happened in the detention room?"

"I'm not sure I remember," Joe replied. He looked at Bob. Bob winked at him.

Sheriff Marshall quickly looked over at Bob. Bob shrugged his shoulders and smiled. "Don't ask me. I wasn't even there."

"Did Don Earl attack you and Deputy Barnes?" the sheriff demanded.

"Somebody attacked us," Joe said.

"Well if it wasn't Don Earl, who was it?" The sheriff's voice was loud and insistent.

"I don't know," Joe said. "I'm new around here."

Sheriff Marshall breathed deeply and exhaled.

"All right, then, just what are you kids doing in Wales?"

Bob raised his hand.

"What?" the sheriff said gruffly.

"We're here on a plant collection project for Dr. James our botany teacher," Bob said, without pausing for a breath.

"You're doing what?"

Joe smiled. This time, there was no pain. "It's like we told you at the Atomic Drive-in: Dr. James is our botany teacher at Ponce de Leon High School. We're staying at the old biological station just outside of town. We're here to survey the area, collect indigenous plants, and then key them for Dr. James."

Sheriff Marshall pushed his hat on the back of his head and scratched his forehead. "Sounds like a bunch of hooey to me."

"It's true, Marshall Sheriff," Bob said. The big man glared at Bob. "I mean, Sheriff Marshall."

"What kind of hat is that?" the sheriff asked, pointing at the top of Bob's head.

"It's a yacht captain's hat," Bob said with pride.

"Well, we don't have any yachts around here. Besides, it looks like it needs to be put out of its misery."

Sheriff Marshall looked at Joe. "What were you doing at the police station talking with Don Earl?"

"I had read about the case in the newspapers," Joe responded. "We have a club at school that studies crimes. I thought it would be cool to talk with Don Earl and report back to the club's members."

The sheriff turned to Bob. "Mrs. Braddock says you and that other girl were at her home, talking to Gayle. Why?"

"Same thing as him," Bob said, thumbing toward Joe.

"How long are you going to be at the biological station?" the sheriff said.

"Through Sunday," Joe answered.

"I'll be out first thing in the morning. Maybe your memory will have cleared up by then." He turned to leave, then stopped. "Oh, yeah," he said, turning around. "Here." He held up a large tennis shoe. "The ambulance guys left this at the police station." He tossed the shoe at Bob. Bob caught it and handed it to Joe. Sheriff Marshall left the room, his heavy footfalls echoing down the hospital corridor.

"Barney Fife and Deputy Dawg all in one package," Bob said when he was sure the man was out of earshot. He turned back to his friend. "So, what happened?"

"Don Earl is the Wolf Man," Joe said without hesitation.

"I figured as much."

"What did you two learn?"

"Gayle says they were attacked by a giant wolf and that Don was defending her. She doesn't know where the carnival worker came from. She passed out just as Don was hitting the wolf with her buckle."

"Did you and Nina tell her about the Wolf Man?"

"No. We didn't get a chance," Bob said. "She's so defensive about Don that I wonder if we shouldn't keep her in the dark, so to speak."

"Interesting choice of words," Joe said. He slowly sat up and put on his shoe.

"Let me help you," Bob said. He lifted one of Joe's arms and draped it across his shoulder.

Joe hopped down. "That doesn't feel good."

"What?" Bob said, panic in his voice.

"A sharp pain right up the middle of my spine."

"Maybe you ought to lie down."

"No. Let's find Nina and get out of here."

"I'm right here," Nina said, entering the room.

"Where's Gayle?" Bob said.

"She went home with her mother." She held up a small square of paper. "I got her number; she wants to talk later."

"Cool," Bob said, reaching for the paper.

Nina jerked the paper away from Bob. "She wants to talk to me. *You* just keep your eyes in your skull, okay?"

Bob grumbled and then helped Joe to a wheelchair. It took all his strength to steady his friend so that he sat easily in the chair.

"Man, you're heavy," Bob said, huffing.

"You should have gotten a look at Don after he

turned into the Wolf Man. At least seven feet tall and three hundred pounds."

"You're certain the Wolf Man has made his appearance?" Nina said as they walked down the corridor.

"Yes," Joe replied.

"What do we know about the Wolf Man?"

"In the movie, he wants to kill the one he loves," Bob said.

"I don't like the sound of that," Nina said.

Bob pushed Joe through the emergency doors. The chilly night air swirled around them as they made their way to Nina's convertible.

"You brought the camera, right?" Bob said.

"Yes," Joe replied. "But it's at the cabin. If I had had it with me, I could have sent the Wolf Man back quickly. Now we have to find Don and convince him to let us videotape him."

"One of us should always have the camera at all times," Nina said. "It's a rule."

Bob sighed. "I knew letting her into the Forensic Club would be trouble. Now we're going to have to put up with a bunch of rules!"

Nina smiled. "Yes, and you're going to have to brush your teeth and wash behind your ears."

"Oh, brother," Bob said with a grimace.

CHAPTER SIX
Central Florida
University Biological Station

They returned to the biological station's cabin shortly before nine P.M. When they had first arrived, they had had only enough time to unpack the car and then head out to their respective assignments. Now they took a good, long inventory of the biological station's cabin.

Bob wasn't disappointed. He was heartbroken. The cabin was beyond primitive. Prehistoric was the word that leaped to Bob's mind. Not only did the cabin not have 500 cable channels, it didn't have a television at all.

The lack of a television — visual lobotomy, as Joe called it — was just the beginning of a couple of hours of whining from Captain Bob, monster hunter and killer.

Whine number two came with the discovery that all six bunk beds were missing their mattresses. Antique, rusted metal springs were on each bed. Many were broken; few had held their spiral flexibility. The monster hunters would be sleeping on the hardwood floor.

Which was whine number three from Captain Bob. The floor was covered in a fine layer of dust and grime.

While the cabin had a sink, a tub, and running water, it lacked an indoor toilet. Joe had announced that he could see an outhouse through the cabin's lone rear window. That was Bob's fourth whine.

The last whine occurred when Bob discovered that the cabin was absent anything that could be consumed by human beings. Bob had tried to cajole Nina into driving back to town to make a quick visit to the Atomic Drive-in, but she had refused, claiming exhaustion and a lack of hunger.

After that Bob fell silent.

"Now, back to business," Nina said, once Bob had ceased his litany of complaints. "If I remember correctly, in the movie *The Wolf Man*, a man by the name of Larry Talbot goes back to his ancestral home in England. He flirts with a girl named Gwen and takes her to see a gypsy fortune-teller. The girl brings along a girlfriend named Jenny. While Larry and Gwen are flirting in the woods, Jenny is frightened by the gypsy fortune-teller, who sees a pentagram on the palm of her hand."

"Hey," Bob said suddenly. "Did you know that the guy who played the gypsy's son in *The Wolf Man* is the same guy who played Count Dracula in *Dracula*?

"Yeah, you're right," Joe chimed in. "That's pretty cool."

"Yeah, because it's the gypsy who's the original werewolf," Bob said, speaking faster and excitedly. "He turns into the werewolf, kills Jenny, and then Larry Talbot kills the werewolf with this cane that has a big silver handle in the shape of a wolf's head."

"But not before Talbot is bitten by the werewolf," Joe added.

"Yeah, transferring the cursed blood of the werewolf to the next man who would turn into the werewolf."

"What was that saying everyone kept repeating?" Nina said.

"Even a man who is pure in heart and says his prayers by night may become a wolf when the wolfbane blooms and the autumn moon is bright," Bob recited, a faraway gleam in his eyes.

"What's wolfbane?" asked Nina.

"We've got some with us," Bob opened his backpack and dug around inside. "It's a poisonous weed. It's like werewolf kryptonite."

"What?" Nina sniffed. "I thought I smelled something stinky from the backseat on the way here. I thought you just hadn't bathed for a couple of days."

"Very funny." Bob grabbed his stomach and laughed a deep mocking laugh. "We'll probably all stink by the time we get out of here, what with the excellent facilities and all." Bob returned his attention to the backpack. He finally gave up and just dumped the contents onto the dusty and grimy floor. "Here it is."

He held up three long brown and brittle stalks that had six blossoms on each. The flowers were a brownish white. Some dead petals fell to the floor. Bob picked up the fallen petals. "Anybody got any tape?"

"Peeee-uuuuu," Nina protested, holding her hands over her mouth and nose. "And I do mean *YOU*, Bob Hardin. Why did you bring that weed?"

"This stinky weed will help save your precious hides when we confront the Wolf Man." He stood and held the brittle stalks in front of him. "Wolfbane, also known as wolfsbane, also known as monkshood because of the hoodlike quality of its flower. Of the genus *Aconitum*: a toxic plant relatively safe for humans if handled properly, but poisonous for animals, especially *Canis lupus*, known to the layperson —" Bob looked at Nina and raised a knowing eyebrow "— as *wolf*. Wolfbane is most deadly to those creatures known as *Lycanthropes*, known to the layperson —" Bob looked at Nina again for maximum impact — "as —"

"Werewolves," Joe finished.

Bob glared at Joe like a child who had just had his balloon popped by the class bully. He sat back on the weak and broken springs of one of the bunks.

"Okay," Nina said. "But put it in a plastic bag or one of the plant presses. This place stinks enough without that weed being waved all over the place.

"So, back to the subject at hand," she continued. "When Dracula appeared, he came disguised as a dentist, not a count or rich person. That was different from the movie."

"Yeah, but we found him in the *Carfax* Hotel, which is similar to the movie because Count Dracula lived at the *Carfax* Abbey in London," Joe said.

"So, maybe each monster will appear a little differently, but there will be some similarities as well, clues to help us find and destroy the monster," Nina said. She looked at the boys. "Any similarities between *The Wolf Man* and what's been happening in Wales, Florida?"

They sat silently for a few moments.

Then Bob said, "The location."

"What do you mean?" Nina said. "Larry Talbot goes back to his father's castle in England."

"No, he doesn't," Bob said slowly. "Larry Talbot goes back to his father's castle located in a small village in *Wales*."

A cold shudder tap-danced up Nina's spine. "That's spooky."

"Also, the fortune-teller saw a pentagram on Jenny's hand, but according to both Don and Gayle, the shaman saw a pentagram on Don's forehead," Joe added.

"Close enough," Bob said.

"Anything else?" Nina said.

They sat in silence for a few minutes.

"Then I guess we can safely assume that we have found the escaped Wolf Man in Wales, Florida?" Nina looked from Joe to Bob.

"Yeah," Bob said. "There's just one problem."

"What's that?" Nina said.

"In the movie, the gypsy werewolf is killed by Larry Talbot. Larry Talbot is bitten and then becomes a werewolf. Larry Talbot then tries to kill Gwen, the girl he loves, but his father, Sir John Talbot, kills him with the cane with the silver wolf head." Bob bounced slowly up and down on the springs, a metallic, rusty squeak keeping time with each bounce.

Joe sat up. "Don was attacked by the carnival barker, the werewolf. Don Earl was bitten. Don Earl transformed into a werewolf."

Nina gasped.

"Yep," Captain Bob said. "That means he will try to kill Gayle. So in order to send the Wolf Man back into the movie, we'll have to kill Don Earl."

Nina picked up her cell phone and punched in Gayle's number. "Stop that, Bob," she scolded as Bob continued to bounce up and down on the rusty metal springs.

"Hello, Gayle?" Nina said into the phone. "Oh, I'm sorry, Mrs. Braddock. Is Gayle there?"

"What's she saying?" Bob said, bouncing up from the bunk bed and standing beside Nina.

Nina ignored him. "Okay. We just wanted to make sure she was okay. Do you want anybody to stay with her tonight? I can come over — oh. Okay. Good night."

"What?" Bob said with sigh.

"Gayle's in bed already and asleep. Mr. Braddock is home now."

"Yeah, but they don't know what we know," Bob said.

"If we tell them, they'll lock us up," Joe said.

"This doesn't make sense," Nina said. "Count Dracula appeared in a whole new disguise. He wasn't *real*. Dr. Dunn never existed before Count Dracula escaped his movie. But, Don Earl Abernathy is a real person. He hasn't just appeared conveniently out of nowhere. We can't just kill him. I mean, there are real consequences here."

Joe yawned. "Maybe we won't have to kill him." He stretched. "Remember: we have to capture the *original* monster, not the ones the monster has attacked. Don has become a werewolf, but it's the carnival barker that's the real werewolf."

"So maybe we won't have to kill Don Earl after all," Nina put in.

"Yeah," Bob said. He reached into his backpack and pulled out one of the peanut-butter-and-bologna sandwiches he had packed for emergencies. He unwrapped it and took a big bite. "We need to talk to the carnival barker. You know these carnival types: drifters who go from town to town."

He smacked his lips. "Bet ya no one's ever heard of this John Winokea before the carnival came to town."

"He's the key," Joe added.

"Yeah, well, I say we feed him one of Bob's sandwiches," Nina said. "That's enough to make anybody want to leave this planet."

Bob smacked his lips again. "Got milk?"

CHAPTER SEVEN
Same Night, Midnight

Gayle was tired, but sleep would not come. She had tossed and turned for over two hours. Her father had come home but had left again when Sheriff Marshall asked him to "hunt for Don." Those were the sheriff's exact words.

Her mother had gone over the Abernathy house to comfort Mrs. Abernathy. Gayle wished she had stayed home. If her mother were here, at least she would have someone to talk to, someone to comfort *her*.

And where was Don Earl? She hoped that her father and Mr. Abernathy would find him first. She had no doubt that Sheriff Marshall would shoot first and ask questions later.

The sheriff had told her in no uncertain terms that Don Earl was dangerous and was to be approached with caution. Sheriff Marshall had dismissed Deputy Barnes's story that a giant wolf had attacked him and the teenager. Unfortunately, he didn't have much respect for his own deputy.

Gayle had pleaded with Sheriff Marshall that

Don would turn himself in, that there was no reason to have an armed manhunt. But her pleas had fallen on uncaring ears.

Gayle sighed, turned onto her side, and grabbed the large gorilla Don had won for her at the fair a month earlier. She hugged it tight. Those happy days seemed so long ago now.

She heard a whine and started, sitting up quickly. Two luminous eyes stared at her in the dimness of the room.

"Snow," she said softly. She let loose the stuffed gorilla and threw her arms around the white-and-gray Siberian husky. Another present from Don Earl, a birthday present. Last year. But now it seemed eons ago.

"Where is Don, Snow? Huh, girl? Where is he?"

The large husky responded with a hefty wag of her tail.

"Maybe we should go look for him, huh, girl? Do you think?"

The husky yelped, then flicked out her tongue to lick Gayle's cheek.

"*Yuck!*" she said with a laugh. "You know I can't stand that, you *bad* girl."

At the sound of the word *bad*, Snow whined and looked up with hurt eyes that begged forgiveness.

"Okay," Gayle said. She threw her arms around the thick furry neck. "I forgive you." She breathed deeply and let the air out slowly. Her head rested on top of Snow's broad skull. "Where is Don Earl?"

A brilliant flash washed the room in stunning white light.

"What?" Gayle gasped, sitting up in bed.

Snow barked and ran to the window.

"Oh," she said as she sat back down. "It's just the security lights. Probably just a raccoon or rabbit." She laid back onto her bed. "Come here, Snow." She patted the side of the bed.

Snow stood at the window on her hind legs, her front paws pressed against the glass. Her head bobbed back and forth.

"Get off that window. I don't want to clean off your paw prints in the middle of the night."

Snow growled.

"Don't take that tone with me, young lady."

Snow growled again. Not the playful growl Gayle was used to hearing when she and her dog would wrestle in the yard. This growl was low and lasted for several seconds. It was a warning, an alarm that danger was near.

Gayle jumped from her bed and ran to the window. "What is it, girl?"

Her window faced the backyard of the Braddock ranch home. The security lights were 500-watt halogen bulbs that washed the color out of everything. Nothing could escape its brilliant glare.

Gayle glanced around the yard, pressing her face against the windowpane to look as far as she could first to the left and then to the right. She gasped and squealed as a rabbit darted across the lawn. Then she laughed.

"You silly girl," she said to Snow, grabbing the dog's ears. "Ain't nothing out there but an old rabbit. Let's go back to bed." She slipped a finger under Snow's pink collar and tried to pull the dog away from the window.

Snow refused to move.

"Okay. We'll just sit and look out the window."

Gayle looked across the back lawn of her home. Her life up until a month earlier had been a happy one, full of hopes and dreams. She and Don Earl would graduate at the end of the year. They were headed for different schools — he to Oklahoma State University on a rodeo scholarship, and she to Florida State University to study animal science. But if their love was true and certain, the distance wouldn't matter.

She looked up at the full moon. The usually creamy surface was washed with a rusty tint. Even the dark valleys of the night's eye were marked with a ruddy complexion. *Almost like blood*, Gayle thought.

Then a memory flashed though her mind like lightning.

She and Don Earl are deep in the Ocala National Forest. They are hunting at night. Not hunting as others do — Don doesn't believe in hunting for sport, and they buy the food they need. No, Don Earl's idea of

hunting is to take a camera with a large telephoto lens mounted on a gun stock and photograph wildlife in all its natural glory.

This hunting trip is special. Don has brought some extra-sensitive infrared film — film that records the heat of objects rather than the light they reflect. Don and Gayle are recording the nocturnal habits of the wildlife in Ocala National Forest. They expose several rolls of film.

Don points to the full moon. It's a moon whose creamy texture has been stained with a rusty hue, a dark bloodred hue.

"That's a Blood Moon," Don Earl says.

"What's a Blood Moon?"

"The Ocala believe that a Blood Moon is an omen. If two people stand beneath the Blood Moon and vow to be true and to love no other, their souls are joined forever."

"Do you think it's just a myth?" Gayle says.

Don Earl puts the camera on the ground and takes Gayle's hands in both of his. "I do beneath this Blood Moon promise my troth to thee and love thee from this point in time and this place in space for as long as the rivers flow and the grass grows and the spirit walks the earth." He leans forward and kisses her on the forehead.

Gayle repeats the vow. She stands on tiptoe to kiss Don's forehead.

They look at each other and laugh. Their laughter echoes off the trees and dark leaves of the Ocala National Forest.

"However," Don Earl says, a bit of warning in his voice. *"There is a caution: According to the legend, if at anytime one of the people breaks this solemn vow, the breaker of vow is condemned to roam the earth as a skinwalker, neither human nor beast, and this half-human, half-beast is tormented to find his true love and convert her into a skinwalker, too.*

Skinwalker! That's what the old shaman had said to Don Earl the night they were attacked by the giant wolf.

They had lived in Wales all of their lives. They had grown up listening to the Ocala legends. The legend of the skinwalker was the scariest. A skinwalker was a man who donned the skin of an animal and chanted ancient and sacred words so that he would literally become the animal whose skin he wore. In this way, the human would become a brother to the animal and the animal would protect him.

Neither Don nor Gayle believed in such tales. They made for a good scare on Halloween or at parties, but no one put any stock in them.

But maybe, just maybe, Gayle reflected, maybe Don Earl has suffered a nervous breakdown and he really believes the old Ocala legend and thinks he is a skinwalker — a werewolf!

If he did, he would go to the Ocala National Forest. That's where he would go. He would go to stand once more in the ancient and primeval Ocala forest beneath the Blood Moon.

Snow growled, a long growl of warning, except this time it ended with a loud bark.

"Snow!" Gayle admonished. "I know where Don Earl is." She grabbed the jeans and shirt she had thrown onto her vanity after returning home from the hospital.

Snow growled and barked again.

"Snow!" She was dressed in less than half a minute.

The window shattered. Gayle screamed and fell to the bedroom floor. Snow tumbled backward and smashed into Gayle's vanity, splitting it in two. Shards of mirror flew in all directions.

The dog was on her feet immediately, leaping toward Gayle.

"No, Snow!" Gayle yelled. She ducked.

The dog sailed over her. The room was filled with the sounds of snarling.

Gayle turned to see Snow facing off with a giant wolf. Except the wolf was standing on its hind legs and had Snow gripped about the throat in its front paws — or were they hands? Either way, they were black and hairy with long sharp claws like the talons of an eagle. Snow was gnashing her teeth, trying to bite the flesh of one of the wolf's arms.

"No!" Gayle screamed. She crawled to her nightstand, threw open a drawer, and dug around inside. Her hand found what she was looking for. She jumped to her feet and ran to Snow. She pressed on the nozzle and filled the wolf's eyes with pepper spray.

The wolf howled and let go of Snow. It backed against the wall as it rubbed its eyes. Gayle followed, continuing to spray the pepper at the wolf.

Snow leaped at the wolf and sunk her teeth into its left thigh. The wolf brought a fist down on Snow's head. The husky yelped, fell to the floor, and didn't move again. The wolf backhanded Gayle with its other hand. The pepper spray flew from Gayle's hand, as she slammed into the floor.

The wolf slowly lowered itself onto all fours. Now it resembled more of a wolf than a man. What was it Nina had called it? A werewolf?

Gayle froze. She wanted to move, but she could not. Every muscle in her body was petrified. She stared into the red eyes of the werewolf. It hovered over her. Its black lips were drawn back to reveal large, pointed teeth dripping with saliva. Gayle tried to speak, to scream, but she could only grunt and gasp for air.

Fear had clutched her in its icy grip, and she felt the warmth of life being drained slowly from her body.

The werewolf lowered its head, the teeth inching closer to her throat.

Tears welled in Gayle's eyes and then trickled down the sides of her face. They were cold and warm all at the same time.

With one last effort, Gayle made a sound. But it wasn't a scream. It wasn't a plea for help. It wasn't a cry for mercy.

"Don Earl," she whispered lovingly.

A warm, comforting blackness wrapped itself around Gayle. She closed her eyes, forgetting about the werewolf whose teeth would soon crush her throat, and fell peacefully into the soothing and eternal arms of death.

CHAPTER EIGHT
Saturday Morning, 5:35

Nina wasn't sure she had heard anything. Maybe she had been dreaming. Maybe some nocturnal animal was rummaging about outside looking for food. Maybe Captain Bob had snorted in his sleep. Nina wasn't sure. Whatever the cause, she *was* sure that she was now wide awake.

Maybe it was just nerves. Joe being attacked had left an unsettled feeling in the pit of her stomach. And Gayle's persistent denial that Don Earl had attacked Joe and the guard made her worry about whether they could rely on Gayle's help.

Or perhaps it was just sleeping on a hard floor in a smelly sleeping bag. What was it she had read somewhere? Often the simplest answer is the correct answer.

Or maybe it was the fact that the fire in the fireplace was little more than embers, and the chill from outside had crept into the cabin.

That's it, Nina thought. *My feet are cold.*

She chided herself and rolled out of the sleeping

bag. She pressed a button on her wristwatch. The LED crystal glowed an eerie blue. The time was 5:35 A.M.

This is way too early for the early bird, Nina reflected.

She pulled on a pair of socks and walked over to the dying fire. Despite her sweatpants and heavy sweatshirt, Nina was still cold. She picked up some small, thin twigs and began breaking them in two, tossing them on the red-hot embers. She blew gently on the fire. Several of the twigs glowed and then ignited, crackling and popping into flames. She grabbed larger, thicker twigs and then placed them on top.

A creaking sound filled the cabin. Nina turned quickly, gasping. An old woman sat in the rocking chair just past the fireplace. Nina cried out in surprise.

"What?" Bob started awake.

"Who?" Joe yelled.

They both jumped up from the hard floor, shouting and bumping into each other.

"Nina?" Bob said.

"What's going on?" Joe demanded, confused.

Nina was already on her feet. She groped along the wall until her hand hit the light switch. Light bathed the room.

"Hey!" Bob shouted, throwing his arms across his eyes. "That hurts!"

"Give us some warning next time," Joe chimed in.

"We've got company, fellas," Nina said. Nina stared at the old woman sitting in the old rocking chair. Her hair was dark gray and her face was brown and wrinkled with deep fleshy wrinkles that folded over one another. Nina had seen such wrinkles on the worn and leathery faces on older people who had worked their entire lives in the sun and weather. What caught Nina's eye was the woman's right eye. While her left eye was clear and a deep brown, her right eye was an opaque, milky white. It did not move when the left eyed moved. It remained still. Still and staring at Nina.

"Where did she come from?" Bob said, still rubbing his eyes.

"How did she get in here?" Joe said, blinking rapidly.

The old woman rocked the chair back and forth.

Nina took a step toward her. "Who are you?" she said softly.

"My name is Wilma Winokea, and I have come to warn you that you are in danger."

"Yeah, from old ladies who sneak into people's houses and scare them to death!" Bob said.

"Be quiet, Bob," Nina said. She turned back to the woman. "Why do you want to warn us? You don't even know us."

The old woman smiled. "Yes, I do, my dear. I knew you before you came to Ocala." She held up a small fur pouch cinched at the top with leather string. "I am a shaman and my tokens told me you were coming here."

"Did they tell you you shouldn't bust into people's homes in the middle of the night?" Bob said.

The old woman ignored Bob. She placed the fur pouch in her lap and rocked for a few moments.

"What else did your tokens tell you?" Nina said, her tone softening.

"The funny thing about tokens. As with words, tokens do not have one set of meanings. Sometimes they mean one thing. Sometimes they mean something else."

"What did your tokens tell you this time?" Nina said.

"That you will meet with Death," Wilma answered without hesitation.

"Whoa," Bob said, raising his hands in protest. "That's not the way I like to greet my mornings!"

"Meet death," Nina repeated. "Do you mean we will die, or witness someone else's death?"

Wilma smiled and stood up. She was a short, heavyset woman, but her skirt was long and dragged on the floor. It was faded, but Nina could tell that at one time it had shone forth with a myriad of bright colors. The yellow shirt she wore was old and faded also. She stepped toward Nina.

"Watch her, Nina," Bob warned. "She's gonna hit you with that furry thing."

Nina frowned at Bob, then looked back at the old woman.

Wilma lifted her hands, palms up. Nina stood for a moment and then placed her hands in the old woman's hands. The shaman spoke an ancient and all-but-forgotten language. Nina felt a surge of energy flow through her.

"What's she saying?" Bob said anxiously.

"Quiet," Joe said to Bob.

A moment later, the shaman had finished her chant and returned to the rocking chair. She looked at Nina. "You understand many things that others cannot," she said, glancing at Bob. "I will tell you about the death you will meet.

"I am a shaman of the Ocala people. We once ruled the land from here to the sea. We were a proud people, but our pride became too great, and we lost our land when the Spanish came. We were given but a little of our once great nation."

"The Ocala Reservation," Nina said.

"Yes, that is all we have. We old ones have learned to live in peace with our destiny. But our younger ones are rebellious and not respectful of the Elder Council. Some say that they wish to regain the land that was stolen from our ancestors. The Elder Council only wants to live in peace. One of the younger ones had a loud and strong voice. Many listened to him. He was the descendant of many great warriors and chiefs and believed it was his destiny to bring honor and glory back to his people.

"One day he was found deep in the Ocala forest, performing an ancient ritual that had long ago been forbidden by the Elder Council. When we found him, he had placed the skin of a wolf over him. The Blood Moon had just risen. He had spoken the enchanted words. We had discovered his heresy too late. He had become a *skinwalker.*"

"What?" Bob said.

"Our people believe we have within each of us an animal spirit. After much meditation, the animal spirit comes to a person and is revealed. To become one with his animal spirit, a person wears the skin of that animal and is transformed into the animal. He then has the power of both the animal and a human. A skinwalker is powerful. He can help his people with the knowledge of the animal spirit. A skinwalker can also use his powers for evil. Just as my son has done.

"Even a man who is pure in heart and says his prayers by night may become a wolf when the wolfbane blooms and the autumn moon is bright."

"Hey!" Bob said. "That's what Gayle said that crazy fortune-teller said to Don Earl."

"Bob! Don't be so rude!" Nina glared at Bob.

Bob looked at her with his best *What did I do?* look. Then he looked at the old woman. His eyes widened and he swallowed hard. "Oh, sorry."

"Smooth move, Captain Boob," Joe said with a frown.

"I have awaited your coming," the shaman said

to Nina, ignoring Bob. "My tokens have told me that you would come to put a stop to the evil."

Nina fixed her eyes on the old woman, listening intently.

"Death has come from the skinwalker that walks the Ocala land," the shaman continued. "His heresy has brought evil to the Ocala and to all who live near us. We tried to capture him, to reverse the spell, but he escaped into the forest. Our ways are ancient. Now we must rely on the new ways to destroy this evil. You," she said, pointing at Nina. "You will help us to be rid of this evil." The shaman drew a deep breath.

Nina knelt beside the shaman. Tears began to fall from the old woman's eyes — the good eye and the bad eye. Nina took her hand.

"And the only way to end the evil is to kill him."

"Kill who?" Nina said.

"My son," Wilma said, and she stared into the fire.

CHAPTER NINE
Two Hours Later

"This doesn't make a lot of sense," Bob said from the backseat of Nina's Camaro.

"Why not?" Joe said.

"Wilma's story about her son becoming a skin-walker: This doesn't fit in with the story of *The Wolf Man*. According to our theory, the monsters appear and take on a new identity, just like Count Dracula did when he became Dr. Dunn, the vampire dentist."

"Yeah," Joe said.

"So, if each monster is to appear and take on a new identity, then Wilma's son cannot be the Wolf Man."

"Because Wilma's son has been alive and kicking for over thirty years," Joe finished.

"Exactly," Bob said.

"Of course," Nina said, "our theory could be wrong. Maybe each monster will manifest itself in a different way. Nothing ever really happens exactly the same way twice. You know the adage of lightning striking twice, right?"

Bob sighed. "I hate it when she throws logic into the mix."

"She could be right," Joe said. "Wilma's son is the carnival barker that Don is accused of trying to kill. That throws your theory about the carnival barker being a drifter right out the window."

"Wait a minute," Bob said, sitting up. "Just a moment ago, you were agreeing with me. Now you're agreeing with her. Which is it, ol' buddy?"

"Actually, all I said to you was 'yeah.' It's usually easier to let you talk than try to argue with you."

"Thanks, ol' buddy, ol' pal." Bob leaned back in his seat. It was only seven thirty in the morning, but already he wasn't having a good day. First an old shaman woman tells him he's going to meet death. Then his best friend implies that he isn't worth arguing with. "Did you bring the camera?"

"Yeah," Joe said, grinning. Nina giggled.

"Very funny." Bob stared out the window.

They had driven Wilma back to her home on the Ocala Reservation within the Ocala National Forest. On her advice, they had decided to check up on Gayle.

Bob was more confused than he normally was. Count Dracula had been easy. One monster, one solution. This time, they weren't sure who the monster was, and there was the real possibility that someone might actually get killed in order to stop the werewolf's terror. John Winokea was not just some character who showed up out of nowhere. He was born and raised on the Ocala Reservation, and he had lived there for thirty years. He worked as a barker at the annual carnival. He was nearly beaten to death by Don Earl. And now he lay in a coma at the Wales Community Hospital.

And that whole story about the *skinwalkers* and the young tribal members wanting to regain the glory of the once-noble tribe. None of that had anything to do with *The Wolf Man.* Unlike their run-in with Dracula, the Wolf Man was proving to be more of a puzzle.

Don Earl Abernathy was not just some phantom figure, either. He was born in Wales and had lived all his life in the small rural town. He had parents and friends and a girlfriend he cared about.

Dr. Dunn had appeared from nowhere and was exposed as the film image of Dracula and sent back into his two-dimensional world. Driving a stake through Dracula's heart didn't bother Bob: He knew that it was a part of the script, all make-believe, smoke and mirrors and digitized magic with a modified camcorder. But this time, they might have to actually send someone to the grave for real.

And to complicate things further, they had not just one monster, but two — John Winokea *and* Don Earl Abernathy had both become werewolves.

Bob sighed. Figuring out the square root of pi was less confusing.

Nina pulled up in front of the Braddock ranch house.

"Hope she has an early-morning sense of humor," Bob said as they walked up to the door.

"Farmers get up early," Joe said.

"That's only in the movies," Bob retorted.

"You two knock it off." Nina pressed the doorbell.

They could all hear the four-note chime from inside the house. They waited in silence.

After a couple of minutes, Nina pressed the doorbell again. Silence.

"Maybe she's out plowing the north forty," Bob said. "Being how she's a farmer and all."

"This isn't right," Nina said, ignoring Bob.

"Yeah, we should all be in bed, sleeping," Bob said.

"Joe, take Captain Bob and check around the back."

Bob grunted.

"C'mon, Captain Jolly," Joe said. He grabbed his friend by the arm.

Bob didn't protest. It wouldn't have done any good, anyway. Joe was too strong for Bob to have pulled away. So, he followed his friend around the side to the back of the house.

Bob spotted the open window first. "It's a little chilly to be sleeping with the window open."

They walked closer to the window.

"This window isn't open," Joe said. "It's busted."

They looked at each other, then scrambled to be the first to take a look.

"What a mess," Bob said, peering inside.

Joe was looking over Bob's head. "It's like a stampede of cattle went through here."

"I don't like the looks of that." Bob pointed to a large dark red spot in the middle of the bedroom floor.

"I think we better check on Nina," Joe said.

They were heading back to the front of the house when a scream pierced the still morning air.

CHAPTER TEN
The Braddocks' Living Room

Nina clawed at icy fingers as they tightened around her throat.

"Shoot her! Shoot her!" she heard Bob yelling from somewhere. His voice sounded far away.

Nina continued to struggle against the cold fingers. She stared into the eyes of Gayle Braddock — bright, heartless red eyes that glowered at her.

"Shoot her!" Bob yelled. He ran and leaped at Gayle, hitting her with a full body slam that knocked her off Nina. His hat flew from his head.

Nina gasped and coughed, holding her swollen throat.

Joe aimed the small digital camcorder and pressed the *on* button. He flipped out the preview screen and watched as Bob wrestled with the rodeo queen. Gayle had changed. She was more muscular, more bulky. Her hair was coarse and thick. Her skin was ashen. Her eyes seemed to glow. And her teeth were twice as large and looked twice as sharp.

The "low battery" light blinked.

Great! Joe thought. He stopped the recording and shook the camera, hopping to shake enough energy out of the battery to give the camera time to do its magic. He held the camera up again, turned it on, heard the whir of the gears, and then — nothing.

"Batteries are dead!" he shouted.

"*Yeech!*" Bob squealed. Gayle was on top on him. He was using all his strength to hold back her wrists. But her long fingers were inching toward his throat. Bob wasn't that concerned about Gayle choking him, but he *was* worried that her long, razor-sharp claws would shred his throat like paper.

"A little help over here," Bob called. "These are claws for alarm!"

Joe hastily sat the camera on the floor and ran to help Bob. He grabbed Gayle in a bear hug and lifted her off his friend. He was surprised at how heavy the small girl was. She struggled as she dangled in the air, kicking at Joe's kneecaps. Joe groaned. He tightened his bear hug. A sharp pain cut up the back of his spine like a chainsaw hacking at wood.

Gayle suddenly jerked her head back and smashed Joe on the chin.

Joe was blinded by a sudden burst of light. Then a black curtain folded over him and a maelstrom of stars whirled about. His knees buckled. He struggled to remain standing, to retain his bear hug on

Gayle. He fell to his knees, but he never let go of the struggling girl.

Joe shook his head to clear it. Then Gayle stopped struggling. Her body weight changed, becoming lighter, almost weightless. Joe finally released her, and Gayle tumbled to the floor and did not move.

The whirling stars before Joe's eyes disappeared. Bob and Nina were kneeling beside a prone and listless Gayle.

"Are you okay, buddy?" Bob said.

"Yeah," Joe said. "I think."

Nina pressed two fingers against the side of Gayle's throat.

"Her heartbeat is strong," she said.

"So is her head," Joe added, touching his chin. The flesh felt mushy, like an old apple. "Oww," he said softly. Now he had a bruised chin to match his black eye. Before long, he'd be a poster boy for accident insurance.

Bob lifted one of Gayle's eyelids and then her upper lip. "The eyes and teeth are changed back."

"Look at this," Nina said. She had pulled back one side of Gayle's pajama top to reveal the girl's left shoulder.

"Wow," Bob said. Joe scooted closer.

They were staring at a large series of scars that covered Gayle's shoulder. The whelp of scars was bright pink and stood out a good half inch from Gayle's flesh. Nina traced them with her finger.

"Teeth marks," she announced.

"Large teeth marks," Bob added.

"Like the teeth marks of a large wolf — a were-wolf," Joe concluded.

Bob suddenly turned to Joe. "What happened to the camera?"

"Battery's dead."

"It probably wouldn't have worked, anyway," Nina said. "I have a feeling it only works on the actual monster, not those who that monster has transformed into monsters."

"It was worth a shot," Bob said. He took off his leather jacket and laid it over Gayle. "I thought she was gonna kill both of us."

Gayle sighed deeply. The three teens tensed and then relaxed as Gayle rolled over to her side and continued to sleep.

Nina frowned. "I wonder where her parents are."

"I didn't see any cars parked outside," Joe remarked.

"That's weird," said Nina.

"I'm glad she didn't transform completely into a werewolf," Bob said. "She was hard enough to fight off as a semi-werewolf." He sat back and crossed his legs. "I left the wolfbane at the cabin."

"Why do you think she suddenly changed back?" Joe asked.

"Because the skinwalker is powerless in the light of day."

All three jumped to their feet, spinning around to face the front door.

Wilma stood in the door frame, her small round figure silhouetted against the rising sun.

"What are you doing here?" Bob asked.

"I heard the spirit of the skinwalker howl in the night air, and I knew that death was walking the earth," she answered. With a slight stagger she started toward the sleeping Gayle. She struggled to kneel beside the girl. Nina reached out, gently took the old woman's arm, and guided her to the floor. "Thank you," the old woman said. She placed her brown withered palm on Gayle's forehead and began what sounded like a soft hymn.

Nina, Joe, and Bob watched in silence as Wilma stroked Gayle's face with her palm. Gayle's taut face relaxed, and a smooth serenity washed over the girl.

Wilma's song stopped and the old woman attempted to stand, straining and grunting as she did so. All three teens bent over and helped her.

"The spirits have been kind to her," Wilma said. She sat in a large wing chair.

"Kind?" Bob said. "She was practically a werewolf. Almost killed Nina and me."

The old woman smiled. "If the skinwalker within her had wanted to kill you, it would have." Her voice was unemotional.

"What?" Bob said. He bent over and picked up his yacht captain's hat.

"She is not yet complete," Wilma said. "Her spirit is strong. She is fighting the skinwalker's blood within her."

"I don't understand," Nina said.

"A skinwalker — a werewolf as you call it — attacks for only two reasons: hunger and love. My son attacked the young man and young woman because he was hungry for the taste of flesh and blood. The young woman has the scars of the skinwalker, but not the star."

"Star?" Nina said.

"The pentagram," Bob replied. "The five-pointed star that appears on the victims of the werewolf."

"Her young man had the star," Wilma said. "I saw it the night he was attacked. I warned him to leave, to go home, to seek the protection of the spirits, but he is an unbeliever."

Nina sat in the wing chair next to Wilma. "Why would Don Earl attack Gayle?"

"The skinwalker's blood boils within him like a hot spring," Wilma said. "He must calm the boiling pain with the blood of the innocent. He must either kill to feed his desire for flesh and blood or kill a loved one to appease the disease."

"That's like the movie," Bob said. "Why didn't Don kill her?" Bob asked. He leaned against a wall so he could keep one eye on Gayle and another on the old shaman.

"The skinwalker has within him two opposite forces: one a primitive beast, and the other a hu-

man being. These two forces battle for possession
of the skinwalker's soul. The young unbeliever is
not yet fully a skinwalker or he would have killed
the young woman."

"What stopped him?" Bob said.

"Love," Nina replied without hesitation.

"Oh, brother," Bob said with a smirk. "This
sounds like a soap opera."

"She's right," Joe said. "Remember the movie?
The Wolf Man tried to kill Gwen but couldn't go
through with it."

Bob shrugged. "Well, if the skinwalker, I mean
werewolf, must kill, then that means Don Earl had
to go after another victim."

"Hey!" Joe said suddenly. He grabbed a photo
from the fireplace mantle. "Remember that large
spot of blood in Gayle's bedroom?" He turned the
photo toward his two friends. "Perhaps the werewolf was satisfied with killing this." He pointed to
the gray-and-white husky in the photo. Gayle's
arms were wrapped around its large neck. She was
laughing as the husky tried to lick her face.

"No!" cried Gayle, sitting up. She was looking at
the photo in Joe's hands.

Nina knelt beside her. "Are you okay?"

"It wasn't Don. It was an animal. The same one
who attacked us at the stables. Don wouldn't do
anything to hurt me!" She buried her face in her
hands. Nina put her arms around her.

"Talk about the Queen of Denial," Bob muttered.

"Knock it off, Bob," Nina said.

Wilma stood. "We must leave this place. The skinwalker will return to complete his bloodlust." She started for the door.

"Where are you going?" Bob said.

"Home," the old woman said, without looking back. She walked out the front door. "I am tired."

"Gayle," Nina said softly. "We've got to get you out of here. We can't leave you here alone. Wilma thinks that the werewolf will come back for you." She helped Gayle stand up.

"Werewolf?" Gayle said, her voice cracking. "What are you talking about? There's no such thing as werewolves. Don and I were attacked by a giant wolf. And now Snow —" Her voice broke and she sobbed aloud. Nina helped her to the door.

"Wait, Wilma," Nina called to the shaman. "We'll drive you home."

The old woman looked back at the two girls. "She will stay with me," she said, pointing a withered finger at Gayle. "She will be safe. The skinwalker will not enter the house of a shaman." Wilma opened the front door of Nina's Camaro and seated herself in the passenger seat.

"Shotgun," Bob said as he ran to the car. The old woman looked up at Bob, the opaque eye searing into his soul. "Okay," he said slowly. "You've got shotgun."

Bob hopped in the back of the driver's side and helped Nina put Gayle in the car. Joe sat on her other side as Nina jumped into the driver's seat and fired up the Camaro.

Wilma's house was just inside the Ocala Reservation. Although it was old, it did not look decrepit. The front yard was an explosion of bright flowers in sharp contrast to the faded brown asphalt siding.

"You must stay, also," Wilma told the teenagers as they climbed out of the car.

"We have a cabin just outside the reservation," Bob said.

"It will not protect you." She stepped slowly up onto the porch, opened the door, and went inside.

Bob looked at the others. "I say we stay at our cabin. I have more faith in my wolfbane than her bag of dirt and bones."

"I say we do as Wilma suggests," Nina said, guiding Gayle up the stairs. "She knows more about this than we do. Besides, it's not Don Earl we're after." Gayle followed Wilma into the house while Nina stayed on the porch with the boys.

"Who, then?" Bob said.

"Wilma's son. He's the Wolf Man. We've got to find him and turn the camera on him. When we do, Don will no longer be a werewolf."

"But —" Bob began.

"No, she's right," Joe said, cutting his friend off. "But first we've got to get the battery charged," Joe said, holding up the lifeless camera. "And the charger's back at the cabin."

"I'm staying here with Gayle and Wilma," Nina

said. "I don't want to leave Gayle alone, even for a little while. Who knows what could happen?"

"So, we walk back to the cabin?" Bob said, frowning. "It must be five miles."

"I can drive," Joe said.

"You have your license?" Nina asked.

"No, but I've got my permit and an A in driver's ed."

Nina stared at the tall freshman. She had had her car since last summer. From the time she was ten and saw her first Camaro, she had only one dream: to own one of her own. She had spent the next six years doing odd jobs, baby-sitting, cleaning houses, flipping burgers, and just about anything she could think of to save up for it. The car was a dream — a dream that came after hundreds of hours of hard work. Her parents were rich, but Nina wanted this car to be hers alone. No one else had ever driven it, and as much as she liked and trusted Joe, she just couldn't bring herself to hand the hard-earned keys to her friend.

"It shouldn't take you more than an hour and a half," she said. She looked at her watch. It was ten past ten in the morning. "I'll look after Gayle and meet you at the cabin this afternoon."

Bob groaned.

"Okay," Joe said. "I understand. We all need to get some rest. Tonight is the waning of the full moon."

"I'm gonna be sleepwalking back to the cabin," Bob said.

Wilma appeared in the doorway. She pointed to

a pile of rusted metal next to the house. "You can borrow the bicycles to ride back to your cabin." She disappeared back into the house.

"*Yeech!*" Bob said. Then he shrugged. He ran to the scrap pile ahead of Joe and pulled out the bicycle with the least rust.

"Cool," Joe said. "This is like when we were kids." He hopped on, popped a wheelie, and sped down the road.

"Hey, not so fast, Goliath. My legs aren't as long as yours." Bob's short legs pumped up and down like pistons.

Nina smiled and shook her head. "What does he mean, *when we were kids*?" She went into the house.

The living room was sparse — a well-worn couch and an even more well-worn chair were separated by a small coffee table with a stained finish.

"She sleeps with the spirit of a child," Wilma said. She was sitting in the chair, watching Gayle.

The blond girl was curled up on the couch, breathing softly, her face peaceful and angelic. There was no sign of the terror she had experienced the night before. Across her injured shoulder was a hoop of an intricate weave with a feather dangling in the middle. Nina recognized it as a Native American dream catcher.

"You think the dream catcher will prevent the skinwalker from taking over her spirit?" Nina said.

The shaman smiled. "Perhaps you are a shaman as well?"

Nina returned the smile. "No. But I've studied some Native American customs and beliefs."

Wilma stooped over Gayle, one hand on the young girl's forehead and the other hovering over the dream catcher. Her voice was soft and smooth.

> *"The way you walked was thorny —*
> *Through no fault of your own.*
> *But as the rain enters the soil,*
> *The rivers enter the sea,*
> *So tears run to a predestined end.*
> *Your suffering is over.*
> *Now you will find peace for eternity."*

"That's pretty," Nina said.

"Do you understand?" Wilma said, her good brown left eye scanning Nina's face.

Nina took a deep breath and let the words run through her head. There was something familiar about them, but she was too tired to figure out where she'd heard them before.

Nina appreciated Bob and Joe's technical expertise and their ability to whiz through complicated computer program language. However, sometimes she felt that they lacked *soul*. The boys' solution was to merely find the monster, point the modified camcorder at it, and photo-vacuum it back onto a disk. But she was becoming aware that the Wolf Man was different, that the solution wouldn't be found in all the electronic synapses of a computer.

A little *soul* would be needed with their science this time.

Wilma took Nina by the arm and guided her to a narrow, short hallway, stopping at a door. "You can sleep in here." She opened the door, then returned to her chair.

Nina peered into the room, then looked back at Wilma. She was about to ask the shaman a question when she noticed that the old woman had already fallen asleep, her chest heaving in a steady rhythm of soft, deep breaths.

Nina hesitantly stepped into the room. At first she'd thought it was Wilma's, but pictures of high-priced luxury cars, sports heroes, and bikini-clad models told her that it must belong to Wilma's son. She walked over to a small desk and looked at the books piled on top. A small one entitled *Skinwalker: Chants and Prayers* caught her eye.

She opened the book and glanced quickly through it. A chill swept over her. She turned, startled. The room was empty. Nina put the book down and walked out quickly, closing the door behind her.

She sat and leaned against the couch. She felt safer being near Wilma. She laid her head on the edge of the couch and was soon sound asleep.

CHAPTER ELEVEN
Later That Same Morning
Somewhere in Ocala National Forest

Cold. Intense cold. The type of cold that embeds itself in your bones and creeps slowly along your spine. He groped for his blanket, wanting to pull it up, to cover himself, to warm himself. His hand patted the area around him, but he could not find the blanket.

He tried to open his eyes. They felt as though they were glued shut. He moved his pupils behind the unmoving lids and squeezed the muscles of his face, trying to pop the lids open.

A thin, dull light peeped through the small slit in his eyes. His lids fluttered open. Everything around him was hazy — a misty canvas of green and white against a washed-out blue background. He stretched the muscles around his eyes, trying to strip the sleepiness from them, trying to get them to focus.

The cold snapped at him again, and a shiver whipped through him. He sniffed, the pungent wet scent of earth assailing his senses.

Don Earl Abernathy bolted upright and looked around.

He wasn't at home in bed. Nor was he in his cell at the jail. Trees surrounded him; the midmorning sun reaching through their leafy canopy bathed the forest floor in a soft yellow light.

Don shook his head, rubbed his eyes, and looked around. He recognized the foliage as that of the Ocala National Forest. He had spent many weekends and summers camping and photographing wildlife in the Ocala and knew the forest almost as well as he knew the rodeo arena.

He pushed himself up and almost fell back down. His strong legs had the consistency of overcooked spaghetti, and he had to grab a nearby tree to keep from falling to the ground. He breathed deeply through his mouth. His ribs ached as though a bull had kicked them. His stomach felt as though he had swallowed a large stone.

Then there was the taste in his mouth. A slick, sticky taste that clung to his tongue and the roof of his mouth. He smacked his lips and tried to get rid of it. He spit. But the taste remained.

It was hauntingly familiar. An ancient taste. A taste of primordial appetite. A taste that Don Earl had rejected years earlier and had vowed never to experience again.

Sickness ballooned in his stomach and made its way up his throat. He spit again. A soft, slimy object hit the ground at his feet. Don Earl fought against the nausea raging within him as he put a name to the revolting taste in his mouth and the object lying on the ground: flesh.

Don's mind exploded in a brilliance of bright white light. He closed his eyes against the blinding rays, only to realize that the light came from within.

Just as suddenly, darkness overwhelmed him. Vivid images appeared against the screen of his mind, unfocused at first but soon sharpening to crystal clarity.

He is running on all fours. No longer a human. A dog. No, a wolf. A giant wolf. Much like the giant wolf that had attacked Gayle and him weeks earlier.

He runs with abandon, his jaws slightly open to suck in the air he needs, his tongue slightly protruding through the massive, sharp canine teeth. He is free. His spirit is one with the forest and the beasts of the earth. His senses are acute: He hears all things around him, smells all things around him, sees all things around him.

He is free. A beast whose only rules are the rules of the powerful and the unconquerable. He is a master and the world is his slave.

He is free. Free from all the restrictive rules and moralistic laws of the weaker two-legged creature called human. His energy knows no limitations, his craving knows no stricture, his facility knows no failure.

He is free. Free from all except for that most ancient and most gnawing appetite that grips the pit of his stomach and twists him into a knot of hot-blooded rage. And he knows, instinctively, that the only way to ease the pain of hunger, to cool the hot blood boiling and coursing through his veins, is to feed on human flesh.

Flesh and blood. His existence relies on obtaining flesh and blood.

He runs through the dark forest and finds himself at a dwelling — a familiar dwelling. The dwelling of someone he loves very much.

The home of Gayle. It is her flesh and her blood that he needs. He will bring her into his world, make her free just as he is free, and together they will rule their world.

A horrific battle with a dog, the puny domesticated descendant of the once-great wolf. With ease, he crushes the dog, then turns his full attention to the human female.

He extends to his full height and looks down at the tiny and weak human female. Her eyes are soft. Her skin glows with a ghostly sheen. He places his hands on her shoulders. She doesn't scream. His bloodred eyes hold her in a trance. He bends over and sinks his teeth into her shoulder, just enough to break the skin and taste the blood.

A sudden shudder shoots through his body. He steps back, and the human female falls to the ground in a dead heap.

The werewolf feels as though someone is fighting him. Someone inside trying to fight his way out. A voice echoes through his head. A human voice. A haunting voice that is also familiar to him.

His own voice.

The werewolf raises its head to the ceiling and howls a sharp, ear-piercing howl that shatters the windows of the bedroom.

He looks down at the human female. The ghostly glow is more angelic than before.

He cannot complete the ritual. He cannot turn Gayle into a terrible beast — a werewolf. The human voice inside him demands that he stop, that he leave, that he let the living go on living — as a human.

The werewolf turns. The deep, dark hunger still baits him, still demands to be satisfied. He scoops up the lifeless dog that has attacked him and bolts through the broken window.

Don Earl Abernathy leaned against a tall tree. He stared at his hands: the black of dried blood was caked on his hands and up his arms. Under his fingernails were bits of flesh and coarse gray-and-white fur.

He looked up from his hands at a shape a few yards from him. It is just a lump — a lump of flesh. The white-and-gray fur stained with the same dark dried blood. He was staring at what was left of Snow, Gayle's beloved Siberian husky.

Don Earl stumbled toward the edge of the black

lake. He fell to his knees and began scooping the water into his mouth. The water was foul, but he preferred it to the greasy, fatty taste in his mouth.

Don Earl, the vegetarian, had tasted flesh. And he had enjoyed it.

CHAPTER TWELVE
Late Saturday Afternoon

Captain Bob stood on a ridge, his back to the deep canyon. The werewolf towered over him, its black fur standing on end, its ears set back against its head, its black lips pulled back to reveal large, yellow, blood-stained teeth.

"Take your best shot," Captain Bob said calmly, a slight smile on his face. "You big, overstuffed excuse for a monster!"

The bloodred eyes of the werewolf widened and it snarled, deep and long. It swung a long, thick, beefy arm at Captain Bob, the daggerlike claws aimed at his throat.

Captain Bob ducked and the claws ripped his hat from atop his head. The werewolf tore at the cap, shredding it into small black strips.

A fury erupted within Captain Bob. "I've had enough of you," he said softly but menacingly.

Captain Bob kicked out with his right foot, hitting the werewolf in the stomach. The monster howled as it

doubled over in pain. Captain Bob planted a right cross
on the left side of the werewolf's head. The beast fell to
the ground with a thud and did not move.

"Oh, Captain Bob," came a soft, female voice be-
hind him. It was a voice that was all lemonade and
Dixie.

He turned. The young woman approaching him was
pretty: long blond hair, deep rich blue eyes, creamy
milk-white skin, and an alluring smile.

"Oh, Captain Bob," she repeated as she threw her
arms around his neck. "You're my hero."

"My pleasure," Captain Bob replied nonchalantly, in
his best Rhett Butler voice. He stared into her eyes.
Their heads moved closer together. Their lips parted.

"Hey!"

Captain Bob opened his eyes. The soft female
face before him expanded and contracted, then re-
shaped itself into a round bulldog face with thick
spectacles atop a greasy nose.

"WOW!" Bob shouted.

"Hey, man! You okay?" the man said.

Bob shook his head. "Uh, yeah. Who are you?"

"You have a nightmare?"

"More like I woke up to one." Bob pushed himself up from his sleeping bag and stretched. His
muscles groaned in protest.

"Sheriff Marshall said I was to check up on y'all."

"What? To collect plants?" Bob looked around.
Joe was not in the cabin.

Deputy Barnes laughed, snorting through his nose. "No, man. Just to make sure you're okay."

"Oh, sure. You must be Deputy Barnes." Bob walked over to the sink and turned on the tap. It spurted and belched, and then burst forth in a solid brown spray. Bob quickly turned off the faucet.

So much for roughing it! I'd like to find the guy who plumbed this place and rough him up, Bob thought grumpily.

"So. Everybody okay?" Deputy Barnes pushed his glasses up on his nose.

"We're fine," Bob said, returning to his bedroll. He pulled a water bottle from his backpack and walked back to the sink. He opened the bottle and drank. Then he poured some out on his hands and washed the grime from the old bike's handlebars off his palms.

At least we didn't have to walk. Yeah, right. The choice of riding those rickety old bikes or walking the five miles was like asking a condemned criminal which method of death he prefers. The result is the same.

Bob looked around. *Great,* he thought, *no towel.*

"Here," Deputy Barnes said. He handed Bob a white cloth.

"Thanks," Bob said as he took the cloth, rubbing the water from his hands. He looked more closely at the cloth and realized that it was a used hand-kerchief. Bob sighed and handed the handkerchief back to the young police officer.

"Keep it," he said. "You might need it again."

"Only if I plan on hanging myself," Bob replied. He threw the wet cloth onto the counter. "Where's Joe?"

"He's outside looking at some plants."

Bob walked swiftly to the front door and out into the late afternoon.

"Why didn't you wake me up?" he asked his friend.

Joe was hunkered over a small plant, holding a small but powerful magnifying glass to one eye.

"Hey! Joe!"

Joe started. "What? What's happening? Everything okay?"

Bob frowned. "Yeah, man. I was just trying to get your attention."

"Well, you made me lose count," Joe retorted. "I was counting the pistils and stamens, trying to key this plant, and now I've got to start all over again. You know, this is for your grade."

"Sorry, man. I was just a little rattled."

"Why?"

"I just dried my hands with Deputy Blockhead's used handkerchief."

"Let me guess: You grabbed before you looked."

"Yep."

Joe giggled.

"I appreciate the sympathy, Chuckles. Nina back yet?"

Joe knelt and put the magnifying glass back to his eye. "No."

"I'm starving. I could eat granite."

"Ask Deputy Barnes to take you into town."

"Hey! Yeah. I can do that. Thanks, buddy." Bob spun around and marched back into the cabin. He found Deputy Barnes sitting on one of the metal spring mattresses, bouncing up and down as rusted, stretched, and broken springs squealed in protest.

"Hey, I think I can play a song on these," the deputy said, smiling.

Bob decided not to comment lest he inadvertently ruin his chance for a ride into town.

"Cool. Think you can give me a lift into town, Deputy Barnes? I'm starving."

"Chad."

"What?"

"Call me Chad."

"Oh. Okay."

The deputy continued to bounce.

"Well?"

"Oh, yeah, sure." He bounced hard one last time and was catapulted off the springs. "Let's hit the road, jack!"

Bob followed Chad around the side of the cabin to his police car. Actually, it was more like a police truck — a beat-up 1964 Chevy step side. The hood, roof, and inside of the bed were painted white, while the fenders and sides of the bed were black. An uneven red stripe snaked down the center of the truck's sides. A cherry-red police light sat on the cab's roof like an inflamed pimple. It was dimpled from several BB shots.

Chad hopped into the driver's seat. "Come on, partner. Get in."

Bob slowly opened the door. He wondered if his mother had paid the health insurance premiums for the month.

"She don't look like much," Chad said, rubbing the dash with pride in his voice. "But she'll do sixty in sixty."

"What is that? Sixty miles per hour in sixty minutes?" Bob quipped.

Chad's snorting laugh resonated in the cab of the truck. "Yeah, right, like you got anything faster!"

For a moment, Bob considered hopping on the rusted, rickety bike and taking his chances. He searched his mind for something nice to say.

"Nice paint job," he finally came up with.

"Thanks, man. They had a special on black and white spray paint at the dollar store." Chad turned the key and began kicking the accelerator. He hit the pedal with such force that Bob thought his foot would go through the floorboard.

The engine whined and spurted and groaned and gnashed and hiccuped with such force that the whole cab rocked back and forth. A chaos of clashing metal was followed by an explosion and the acrid smell of gasoline.

"That's my gal!" Chad shouted above the clamor.

He stomped on the clutch pedal and jammed the shift lever up. A metallic gnashing of gear teeth roared above the engine. "Here we go, man!"

The truck lurched forward and spurted to a stop.

Bob just swallowed.

Forty minutes later, Bob walked back into the cabin, a bag of burgers in one hand and a lump in his throat.

"You remember that movie about the car that was possessed and killed all those people?" he asked.

"Uh-huh," Joe said, grabbing a burger and a box of fries from the bag.

"I just rode in its more evil cousin."

Joe's laugh was muffled as he chewed.

"Hey, guys," Chad called, dashing into the cabin. "Just got a call on the radio."

"That thing has a radio?" Bob said incredulously.

Chad snorted and shook his head. "Of course it does. What? You think we just lean our heads out our patrol cars and holler at each other?"

"Well —" Bob began with a shrug.

"What was the call about?" Joe said.

"Sheriff Marshall says he found Gayle's dog in the woods. Looks like it's been through a meat grinder."

"Gayle's not going to like that," Joe said.

"Oh, yeah," Chad added, his face puzzled. "And

that old shaman's boy, John Winokea? He's missing from his coma."

"What did you say?" Bob said.

"John Winokea has apparently recovered and escaped from the hospital," Joe interpreted. "Now we've got two werewolves on the loose!"

CHAPTER THIRTEEN
Same Time
Wilma's House

Nina opened her eyes slowly. Wilma wasn't in her chair. She turned her head slightly. Gayle was still asleep on the couch.

Nina stood and stretched. She looked around the room. From the dim light trying to break through the heavy curtains, Nina guessed that the time was midafternoon. She looked at her watch. She was right. She pulled her cell phone from her pocket and dialed the number for the biological station cabin.

The phone rang several times, and then Joe picked up.

"Hi, Joe. It's Nina."

"Oh, hey. You still at Wilma's?"

"Yeah. What's going on there?"

"Deputy Barnes stopped by to see how we were doing and he took Bob to the Atomic Drive-in. We're eating lunch."

"That sounds good. I haven't eaten anything since last night."

"I'll save you some of mine."

"Thanks, but I'll get my own. Why is Deputy Barnes there?"

"Sheriff Marshall sent him over to check up on us. I think the sheriff wants to know if we know anything."

"Do we know anything?" Nina asked.

"Not any more than we did yesterday."

"So, what's the plan?"

"No plan, Stan."

"I wonder if they've found Don yet."

"No, but they found Gayle's dog. It's not good news."

"I was afraid of that."

"Hey, you know, you ought to call Gayle's parents and tell them where she's at."

"I did that earlier. I guess they spent all night with Don Earl's parents."

"Yeah, they must be pretty upset. And there's more bad news. John Winokea woke up from his coma and escaped from the hospital."

"Oh, no. All right, I'll be over to get you guys in a while."

"We'll be here."

"*Bon appétit!*" she concluded and flipped her phone shut.

"You slept well."

Nina started and spun around. Wilma was sitting at an old aluminum table just inside the kitchen.

"Yes. I did." She joined Wilma at the table. "I have to tell you something. Your son has escaped from the hospital."

Wilma smiled sadly. "I know. That's why I am making dream catchers for you and your friends. They will protect you from the skinwalker." Wilma's fingers were old and thick and weathered but they moved with agility and precision. She had finished one already and was working on a second.

"Can I help you?"

"Yes, I think you can." She put down the dream catcher she was working on and picked up a metal hoop at the end of the table. The hoop was three inches in diameter and solid silver. "Pure evil can only be defeated by pure silver."

"I've heard that before. From Captain Bob."

"Truth is universal," Wilma said, breathing heavily. She picked up a small spool of coarse, thick string. She handed both of them to Nina.

"What do I do?" Nina asked.

"What the spirits guide you to do."

"How do I know what the spirits will guide me to do?"

"Enough talk. Just do."

Wilma picked up the unfinished dream catcher and began twisting the coarse string around the hoop. Nina watched, wanting to imitate Wilma's movements until she could do it on her own. Wilma twisted the string three times around the hoop and then brought the string across to the opposite side, wrapping it three times around the hoop. She repeated this until the hoop was finished.

The completed hoop looked as though a spider had woven a thick web within the circle, but the middle of the circle was left empty.

"Here," Wilma said, putting a weathered brown finger through the center of the dream catcher, "is where the dreams come. The good dreams enter through the perfect center, but the bad dreams are chaos, without direction, and are caught in the web so that the dreamer has only pleasant dreams."

"I understand," Nina said.

"I believe you do," Wilma said with a small smile.

It seemed simple. Nina began imitating Wilma's movements, but within a matter of moments, the hoop was a tangled mass of knotted string. Nina was startled by Wilma's laugh.

"Perhaps you are not a dream weaver, my dear. Perhaps you are what we Ocala call a dream unraveler." She laughed again.

"It looks simple."

"Yes. And it is simple. It is you who are complicated." Wilma picked up another hoop and more string and began weaving around the circle.

Nina concentrated, furrowing her brow and pursing her lips. The old shaman's fingers moved quickly and silently. Wilma began to hum, softly at first and then more loudly.

Nina looked at her hoop and string. She closed

her eyes. She felt the hoop with the fingers of her right hand. She rubbed the coarse string between the fingers of her other hand. A soft orange glow began to replace the darkness behind her eyelids. She smiled. She relaxed her breathing and untensed the muscles around her eyes. The hoop and the string came into focus. She began to weave, not as fast or as precisely as Wilma, but still, she was weaving.

Wilma's humming kept time with Nina's weaving. In a few minutes, Nina's dream catcher was complete. She opened her eyes. The hoop and the string were still in her right and left hands.

"I didn't weave anything," Nina said, puzzled.

"Dream catchers are first created in the world of dreams. Only then can they be created in this world."

Nina smiled. "The spirits will guide me."

"No," Wilma corrected. "The spirits have already guided you. You must now catch up with them before they move on."

Without thinking, Nina began to weave the string around the hoop as she had seen in her waking dream. Ten minutes later, she had created an exact replica of Wilma's dream catcher.

Wilma smiled and resumed her humming.

"Why do you have six hoops, Wilma?" Nina said nonchalantly. She attached a yellow parakeet feather to the center of her dream catcher. "There's me, Joe, Bob, Gayle, and Don Earl. Five. Why six?"

"My son," was all Wilma said.

Nina nodded. "Then we won't have to kill your son as you said earlier?"

"We still must kill him. That is how it is written. He should have died that night during the last Blood Moon."

"What?"

Wilma did not answer. She hummed.

A few moments later, Wilma said, "Like any door or any window, the dream catcher works both ways. I will use my son's dream catcher to snatch the evil spirit within him that turns him into a beast. We can only do this if he is dying. The spirit will try to escape to find a new host in which to project its nightmares."

"But the evil spirit will be caught in the hoop's web," Nina said. "And Joe, Bob, and I will be protected from the evil spirits by our own dream catchers."

"You may have Ocala blood, my young novice," Wilma said.

Nina picked up another hoop and more string and began making a dream catcher for Bob. Next she would make Joe's. Maybe Wilma was right. When the skinwalker spirit escaped from John Winokea, Don, and Gayle, it would seek a new home of horror, and she didn't want Bob or Joe, no matter how much they acted like freshmen, to be possessed by the spirit of the skinwalker.

Maybe the way to defeat the Wolf Man *would*

have more to do with soul than science. Maybe their theories about the camera were wrong. Perhaps each monster would be just as unique and fascinating as each of the six horror films that Bob, Joe, and she enjoyed so much. *And as uniquely difficult to catch,* Nina reflected.

Nina wasn't watching her fingers as they guided the string around the hoop. She didn't have to. She could do it in her sleep. She laughed. She could make dream catchers in her sleep.

Then her eye caught a shape she hadn't seen before. A shape within the dream catcher itself. She had been concentrating so hard on technique that she had not paid attention to the form she was weaving.

A five-pointed star. A pentagram. The sign of the werewolf.

Bits of black-and-white light flashed through her mind. *What was it? What was the memory that was trying to break through the brick wall of stubborn consciousness that kept the dreamworld imprisoned during the light of day?*

A soft, deep voice filled her head. Filled her head because the voice did not come from without, but from within. Nina looked at Wilma, but the old shaman continued her weaving and humming, unaware of the words filling Nina's mind. A thick accent from an ancient land, uttering ancient words whose sole purpose was to ward off evil and keep the innocent still innocent — at least, for one more moment.

An ancient voice, thick with a foreign accent and heavy with foreboding.

You must wear the pentagram. It is a charm against the werewolf, it said in a soft, thick accent. It was the voice of a woman. A woman upon whom the wisdom of the ages had placed a terrible burden.

What was the memory? Why can't it break through? Who was this woman with the burden of good and evil upon her shoulders?

Wilma continued with the catcher of dreams, rocking back and forth in rhythm to her humming and weaving, oblivious to the dark world and the terrors with which it had surrounded her.

CHAPTER FOURTEEN
Saturday Evening
Dusk

Joe picked up the camcorder. "The red light's off, so it's charged."

"What time is it?" Bob said. He walked over to the refrigerator and pulled out a jug of orange juice. He twisted the cap off and drank deeply.

"Hey!" Nina protested. "Use a glass. I don't appreciate drinking your backwash."

Bob gasped and wiped his lips. He screwed the cap back on and put the orange juice back in the refrigerator.

"That was good."

"I'm not drinking out of that," Nina said.

"Suit yourself." Bob rejoined Nina and Joe. "I'm still mad that we had to bicycle five miles back to the cabin when you could have loaned us your car."

"Yeah," Nina said, "I'll remember that the next time you want me to break the law." She rolled her eyes.

"Where's Gayle?" Joe asked.

"She's still at Wilma's. A dream catcher is protecting her."

"A what?" said Bob.

"A dream catcher," Nina replied. "Here's one for each of you." She draped the dream catchers around their necks. "Wear these. They'll protect you from the skinwalker."

"You mean werewolf, right?" Bob said, eyeballing his dream catcher.

"I mean *evil* spirits," Nina replied.

"This is pretty cool," Joe said. "Is this a hawk feather?"

"Yeah. I thought you'd like it."

"You made these?" Joe said.

"Yeah. Wilma taught me."

"What kind of feather is on my dream catcher?" Bob wanted to know.

"A loon," Nina said without hesitation.

"Thanks."

"You're welcome."

"So what's the plan, Stan?" Joe asked.

"We're to go back to Wilma's. All of us," Nina said.

"We better get going," Joe said. "Sun's setting. Moonrise is at seven-fifteen."

"Tonight is the waning of the full moon," Nina said.

"What's that?" Joe said.

"A full moon doesn't just last one night," Nina explained. "It has a beginning, a middle, and an end. The beginning is the waxing and the end is the waning. A skinwalker or werewolf can appear for three nights, during the waxing, the second night, which is actually the full moon, and then the waning. It is the second night, when the full moon is most complete, that the werewolf is most powerful."

Bob reached across the couch and grabbed his backpack. He unzipped it and pulled out his wolfbane. *"Even a man who is pure in heart and says his prayers by night may become a wolf when the wolfbane blooms and the autumn moon is bright,"* he recited.

"Put that stinky thing away," Nina ordered.

"Hey, I'm not going anywhere without my wolfbane," Bob said.

"Maybe that's why you can never get a date," Nina retorted. She turned to Joe. "We've got to get back to Wilma's. It'll be dark soon."

"I'm ready," Joe said, camcorder in hand.

"Me, too," Bob said, tucking the wolfbane in his shirt pocket.

Nina groaned. "Well, you're sitting in the back and we're driving with the top down. I don't want that thing stinking up my car."

They walked out of the cabin into the darkening day.

Wilma was sitting on the front porch in a squeaky rocking chair that looked as though it could fall apart at any second.

"Where's Gayle?" Nina asked as the trio stepped onto the porch.

"She is still sleeping," the old woman said, her left eye moving between each of the three teens. The white, opaque eye remained on Bob. He stared back. He wasn't going to let a crazy old woman scare him. Wilma chuckled.

"What is that?" she asked, pointing to the camcorder in Joe's hand.

"That," Nina began, "is what we use to capture the monsters. Joe modified a digital camera so that it catches the monster's image and vacuums it in. Then we transfer the image back to the monster's movie."

Wilma smiled. "Your machine will not work. My son brought the evil through magic, and through magic only will it be destroyed." She rubbed her forehead. "You must kill the evil."

"No."

Everyone turned. Gayle was standing in the doorway. Bob was surprised to see how pretty she looked after sleeping for nearly twelve hours. He had met her only the day before, and she had looked as though she had been crying for weeks. Now her blond hair was soft and flowed to her shoulders. Her blue eyes were clear, the puffiness gone. She was small, but she stood tall and looked determined.

"You can't kill Don. He's not a monster. He was attacked by a monster. Why does everyone keep forgetting that?"

Nina stepped toward her. "Gayle, Don was attacked; no one is forgetting that. But when a werewolf attacks and bites a victim, the victim is infected with the werewolf's blood, and then the victim becomes a werewolf during a full moon." Nina stepped closer and gently touched Gayle's left shoulder. "You have the scars of a werewolf. You were changing into a werewolf this morning when we arrived. Only the setting of the full moon stopped you completely."

Gayle laughed incredulously. "First you and Bob tell me that Don was attacked by a werewolf. Then you tell me that Don has become a werewolf and attacked me. Now you tell me that I'm a werewolf and attacked you." She shook her head. "You guys have been watching too much TV."

A faded black car with rusty hubcaps pulled up in front of Wilma's house. Sheriff Marshall turned off the engine. The car's springs groaned with relief as the big man got out.

"Gayle, I hate to tell you this, but we've found your dog," the sheriff announced from the bottom of the porch.

"No," Gayle said softly.

"We also found this next to her body." He held up a strip of orange cloth. Joe recognized the material from Don's jailhouse jumpsuit.

Gayle sobbed and buried her face in her hands. Nina put her arms around her.

"If you have any idea where Don is, you ought to tell us before someone gets killed."

Gayle only shook her head.

The sheriff looked at Wilma. "We think your son escaped sometime last night and that he has gone after Don. Do you have any idea where he might be?"

The old woman rocked back and forth. "He is where you cannot reach him."

The sheriff shook his head. "This is no time for riddles. If you know where we can look for him, you should tell us."

Wilma got up and went into the house.

The sheriff looked at the teens. "Gayle. Your parents want you to go home. They're waiting for you. They said to stay away from that old medicine woman."

"I'll drive her," Nina said.

"You three plan on leaving tomorrow, right?" the sheriff said.

"That's the plan," Bob said.

"Well, how about sticking to the plan?" Sheriff Marshall replied. He got back into his car and drove off in a cloud of dust and exhaust.

Wilma came back out onto the porch. She had a shawl around her shoulders. Her pouch of tokens was tied to a sash she wore around her waist. She had placed a dream catcher with the pentagram center around her neck.

"It is time to find the skinwalker and destroy him," she said in a voice that was deep and ancient. Foreign.

Nina frowned. She looked at her friends. Didn't they hear the change in Wilma's voice? It was the same voice she'd heard earlier. *Why can't I remember?* Nina asked herself.

"Doesn't look like anyone's home," Joe noted as Nina stopped her car in front of the Braddocks' ranch home.

The sky had turned a silky blue and the stars were beginning to shine against the dark canvas.

"That's strange," Gayle said. "Sheriff Marshall said my parents were waiting for me at home."

"Maybe they already went to bed," Bob said.

Nina bit her bottom lip. She had been quiet during the ten-minute trip from Wilma's to the Braddock home. But something was gnawing at the back of her brain.

"My folks wouldn't go to bed without seeing if I was okay," Gayle said. She climbed out of the car and walked toward her front door.

Nina, Joe, and Bob exchanged worried glances. Then they followed Gayle onto the porch. Wilma was right behind them.

"I telephoned your parents before we came out here," Wilma said. "They are aware of your safety."

Again, that deep and ancient foreign voice.

Gayle opened the front door and headed up the stairs. "Mom? Dad?"

An icy hand gripped her wrist like a vise.

"Gayle." The voice was weak, raspy, barely audible. *"Gayle. You must help me."*

Gayle stared down into the luminous eyes of a half man, half wolf. Despite the blood-filled hate in those eyes, she recognized a spark of human tenderness. It was her boyfriend, Don Earl.

CHAPTER FIFTEEN

"Gayle!" Nina yelled. "Run!" In two bounds, Nina was on the stairs next to her friend. She grabbed her around the waist and began to drag the girl upward.

"No!" Gayle screamed, clinging to the railing as Nina pulled at her.

"Hey, fuzzy face," Bob called to the werewolf. In his eagerness he pushed Wilma out of the way and ran up the stairs, accidentally knocking the shaman to the ground. "You a vegetarian?" He pulled a stalk of wolfbane from his pocket. "How about some tossed salad?" He pulled a bloom from the stalk and threw it at the monster.

The bloom was withered and brown, but it was heavy. Even in the growing darkness, Bob's aim was true. The wolfbane hit Don Earl on the cheek and stuck to his thick fur. Soon the air was filled with the pungent smell of burning hair.

Don Earl howled — the howl of an animal caught in a trap. He pulled at the flower, smoke rising from his hand as he grasped the poisonous bloom. The bloom exploded into flame as he tossed it on the floor.

"Want a second helping, dog face?" Bob pulled off two more bulbs and threw them at the monster. Both hit their target and burst into flame, burning first the fur and then the flesh of the half wolf, half man.

"NO!" Gayle screamed from the top of the stairs.

Don howled again and knocked the bulbs from his face.

Bob pulled more blooms from the stalk, but before he could throw them, the werewolf had back-handed him, smashing him into the ground.

"Smile!" Joe yelled. "You're on Terror Camera!" He raised the camera and pressed the orange RECORD button. He flipped open the small preview screen and watched the werewolf as it grew larger, taller, the torn and tattered orange prison jumpsuit ripping still more.

Joe continued filming, but nothing was happening. At least not what he wanted to happen. He had clung to the vain hope that whatever was making Don a werewolf would be vacuumed into the camcorder, and Don would return to being wholly and solely human.

But nothing happened. Except that the werewolf grew larger and larger in the preview screen — not because it was still growing, but because it was coming closer and closer to Joe.

The growl erupted into a nuclear bark that threw Joe back through the door. He tripped over the prone body of Captain Bob, and the camera flew from his hand and smashed into the ground. He was out like a light.

"NO!" Gayle yelled.

Nina had to summon all her strength to hold on to the rodeo queen. Gayle's body began to shake and tremble, slowly at first and then vibrating so intensely that Nina lost her grip and stumbled down the stairs. She grabbed on to the railing to keep herself from falling and looked back up at Gayle.

She was no longer Gayle. In a matter of seconds, Gayle had transformed into a werewolf, her luminous red eyes glowing in the gloom at the top of the stairs.

The she-monster began a slow descent toward Nina. Nina moved backward one step at a time. She did not dare take her eyes off the monster, and she did not dare move too quickly for fear she would stumble and fall. She reached the bottom of the stairs and began to back slowly away, toward the open front door.

But she backed right into something large and hairy. Don Earl, werewolf, stared down at her, his hot, fetid breath beating down on her like the heat of a summer day. Gayle, who was by now just as large and just as terrifying as her werewolf boyfriend had reached the bottom of the stairs and stood in front of Nina. Twin rumbling growls reverberated through Nina's trembling body as she stood between the werewolves.

"All right, guys," Nina said to no one in particular, her voice cracking. "This isn't how I imagined dying: not as the main course for two hungry werewolves. Someone do something!"

But the only noise was the rapid but steady growling of the two werewolves. Both boys were still unconscious and Wilma remained motionless where Bob had inadvertently pushed her.

Nina tilted her head back and looked up. "Remember, Don Earl," she said as calmly as she could under the circumstances. "You're a vegetarian."

Gayle reached out with her hand and ran the long sharp black claws over Nina's face. It was just enough for Nina to feel the cold indifference of their razor edges, but not enough to break the skin and draw blood.

Nina tried to keep herself from shaking. She raised her hands to place against her heart, which beat so fast and so hard that it felt like a jackhammer pounding against her chest. Her hand fell on the dream catcher with the pentagram center around her neck.

A voice soft and thick with a foreign accent drowned out the noise in her head. *You must wear the pentagram. It is a charm against the werewolf.* The voice was familiar and yet strange all at the same time.

Nina held the dream catcher out in front of her, toward Gayle.

Gayle backed away, her arms up as if to protect herself. Her bloodred eyes began to fade.

Nina stepped forward.

Gayle stumbled against the stairs. She began to change, to shift back from werewolf to human. A gray mist rose slowly from her body and snaked its way toward the dream catcher. The mist intensified as Gayle became increasingly less wolf and more human. A steady stream hit the woven pentagram, twisting and weaving its way throughout the intricate design, becoming one with the rough string that made up the pentagram.

Moments later, Gayle was completely human. She swayed and fell. Nina lurched forward and caught the rodeo queen before she hit the ground. She laid Gayle gently on the floor at the foot of the stairs.

Nina heard a growl behind her. The other werewolf was still right there. She spun around, holding the dream catcher in front of her.

"All right, dog breath. It's your turn." She thrust the dream catcher toward the werewolf. It snapped at her and swiped at her with its claws. Nina took a deep breath and stepped closer to the monster. The beast backed out the door. It, too, stumbled over the prone body of Captain Bob, and flipped over onto all four legs. It darted off into the black night.

Nina turned and ran back to Gayle. She checked the girl's pulse and breathing. Nina heard a noise behind and turned, holding the dream catcher in front of her.

"He is gone," Wilma said, standing in the door. "He returned to take the one he loves, but he has failed, and now he will seek other blood and flesh to satisfy his ancient hunger."

"What happened?" Bob said, slowly peeling himself off the ground.

"Good thing the camera didn't smash to pieces when I fell," Joe said, joining them. He looked at Wilma and Nina as they sat next to Gayle, who appeared to be sleeping. "What happened?"

Wilma knelt beside the girl, holding a dream catcher over her. She mumbled a chant.

"I thought wearing the dream catcher would protect her," Nina said, still panting hard. "I thought the dream catcher would stop her from becoming a werewolf, would keep Don Earl away from her."

Wilma did not look up. "Dreams are hopes and wishes, and the dream catcher reacts to the desires of the one wearing it. Her love for the boy is strong, so strong that she is willing to become a skinwalker herself to be by his side."

"This sounds more and more like some afternoon horror soap opera," Bob commented.

"Hey, I thought Gayle's parents were supposed to be here," Joe said. "We better make sure Don Earl didn't get them."

"Good idea," Nina said. "Bob, why don't you go with him?"

Bob nodded, and the boys left together.

Wilma continued to lean over Gayle, chanting. Nina smoothed the girl's hot forehead. "Poor kid," she whispered.

Bob and Joe returned a few minutes later. "No one's here," said Joe.

"I bet they went out to look for Don Earl again. But Sheriff Marshall said they'd be home," Bob said. He looked at Joe and frowned. "Know what I'm thinking?"

"I can guess."

"Uh-huh. Sheriff Marshall is involved in this somehow."

"Hey, just how did you defeat the werewolf?" Joe asked Nina.

"The pentagram," she replied. "On the dream catcher. Remember in the movie: It weakens the werewolf, they start to change back. I was able to affect Gayle, but Don got away."

Wilma waved her dream catcher over Gayle and said,

> *"The way you walked was thorny —*
> *Through no fault of your own.*
> *But as the rain enters the soil,*
> *The rivers enter the sea,*
> *So tears run to a predestined end.*
> *Your suffering is over.*
> *Now you will find peace for eternity."*

Wilma finished and bowed her head. She looked as though she had fallen asleep.

"That's the second time she's said that to Gayle," Nina whispered to Bob. "I know I've heard that somewhere before."

"Of course you have," Bob whispered in return. "It's from *The Wolf Man*. The old gypsy woman says it when her son dies and then again when Larry Talbot dies."

"Why is Wilma saying it now?" Nina asked, eyeing the wizened shaman.

"That's a good question," Bob said.

CHAPTER SIXTEEN
One Hour Later
Home of Wilma Winokea

"Every time we have a werewolf around, Wilma seems to be able to bring the situation under control," Nina said. She, Joe, and Bob sat on the porch of Wilma's house. "There must be something to the dream catcher after all. Look how I was able to use it to transform Gayle back to human. And it does have the pentagram shape inside it."

"Ah . . . a force that can be used for good *and* evil," Bob said with mock thoughtfulness, raising one eyebrow.

A sob came from inside the house.

"That girl is cursed," Joe said. "First her boyfriend turns into a werewolf, and now her parents are missing."

"I still say it was a mistake for her to call the sheriff's office," Nina said. "Sheriff Marshall's on my list of people not to trust right now."

"I'll put my faith in this," Bob said. He held up the wolfbane. "Fuzzy Face wasn't too combative when I hit him with the old fastball."

"What are you going to do when you run out of that stuff?" Nina said.

"I'll worry about that *if* it happens." Bob looked at the index finger on his right hand. He had jammed his finger trying to brace his fall, and now it had lost all feeling. He wondered if he was getting any circulation at all. "Hey, Joe." He held up the first finger. "Does my finger look blue to you?"

"No," Joe said, without looking up from the camcorder. "It looks just as happy as the other nine."

"Ho, ho, ho." Bob laughed sarcastically.

"I think the camcorder is okay," Joe announced.

"Good," Nina said. "Didn't work on Don Earl, did it?"

"No."

"Then we know for sure it's Wilma's son we have to get," Nina replied with certainty.

"I still don't get it," Bob said. "*The Wolf Man* isn't following rules. We're supposed to have a monster manifest itself and then we film it and everything goes back to normal. Instead we have two werewolves running around the Ocala National Forest, an old shaman who throws dream catchers at everyone, a deputy who's not allowed to put bullets in his gun, and a sheriff who leads us straight into a trap."

"Wait, let's talk about that for a minute. Why would Sheriff Marshall want to lead us into a trap?" Joe said.

"I'll ask him when we find him," Bob replied.

"I still wonder how Wilma knew that poem from *The Wolf Man*," Nina said.

"Maybe she's a fan, too," Bob said.

"I don't think so," Nina added. "She doesn't even have a television."

"Yeah, but she's old enough to have seen it when it hit theaters in 1941," Bob said.

The door creaked open. Wilma stepped out onto the porch.

"Did Gayle find her parents? Did the sheriff know where they are?" Nina asked her.

The old woman sat in her rocking chair. "No."

"Why would the sheriff lead us into a trap?" Nina said.

"He is Ocala," Wilma said. "He and my son serve on the Elder Council."

"You think Sheriff Marshall is working with your son?" Nina said.

"They spoke often of taking back the land of our ancestors," Wilma replied.

"Do you think they've done something with Gayle's parents?"

Wilma sat silently and rocked in her chair.

"Do you know where they might be?" Nina asked after a few moments. "You told me yesterday that your son performed the ritual of the skin-walker. You also said he had to do that in the Ocala forest. Do you know where?"

"There is a place where the water is black,

where our ancestors would perform many of our tribal rituals. It is a place sacred to us."

"Sounds like the water I took a bath in this morning," Bob said.

"Was the water black before or *after* you took your bath?" Nina asked.

"Hey, hey there. You can make fun of the hat all you want, but I'm very serious about my hygiene," Bob protested.

"Whatever, black-water boy," Nina answered, rolling her eyes. "Would John be there?" she asked Wilma.

Wilma replied, "A skinwalker must return to the ritual site to renew his power."

"He was in a coma for a month," Joe said. "He must be pretty weak."

"I'm beginning to think," Bob added, "that he didn't escape from the hospital. If he and Sheriff Marshall are old friends, maybe the sheriff helped him leave."

"That's an intelligent assumption, Captain Bob," Nina said.

Bob smiled. "Even we madmen have our moments."

"Where is this place of black water?" Nina asked Wilma.

"It is called Deadman's Landing."

"I don't like the sound of that," Bob said.

"Will you tell us how to get there?" Nina said to Wilma.

The old woman ran a hand across her face. "One promise."

"What is it?" Bob said.

"When we find my son, you must destroy him."

Bob swallowed hard. For all his talk of fighting monsters, he had no stomach for actually killing anybody.

"I'm going to have to give my baby a lot of TLC when we get home," Nina said as they drove down a rutted dirt road.

Things had gone from bad to worse. The asphalt road into the Ocala National Forest was filled with potholes, and the dirt road was rutted and dotted with dips.

"Oww!" Bob shouted as he hit his head against the side of the car. Twice his hat had flown off his head until finally he just held it in his hands. The car bounced to the left and right. "You ought to slow down!" Bob shouted. "I feel like I'm going to be seasick."

Joe smiled. "Just imagine you're on a carnival ride."

"I'd rather imagine I'm home playing video games."

The car screeched to a stop.

"That's as far as we go in my car," Nina announced.

Bob hopped out quickly, his legs nearly buckling under him. "I feel like I've been through a blender."

"We're not there yet," Nina said. "We've got to hike about two miles. Wilma says the road was washed out during the last rain."

"Great," Bob said.

"Let's go." Nina started up the path.

The path led them into the edge of the Ocala National Forest. The moon was at a forty-five-degree angle to the earth. The coolness of evening had settled on the forest.

"Wish I brought my coat," Joe said, eyeing Bob's leather jacket.

"Do you think we'll find Don here?" Gayle said.

"He's under the influence of John and the sheriff," Bob said. "The sheriff sent us back to your house knowing that Don was waiting for you."

"But Don asked me to help him," Gayle said.

"His human side was speaking," Wilma said. "He is between two worlds. His mind and spirit are confused."

Bob pulled at Joe's elbow, indicating he should slow down. They let the others walk ahead.

"You think it's wise letting Gayle come with us?" Bob said to Joe.

"Too late now," Joe said. "She's probably safer with us, anyway. We wouldn't want her turning into a werewolf on a bunch of strangers. Plus, why didn't you say something earlier?"

"I can't think of everything," Bob protested. "She turned into a werewolf just like Don. And now she's going to help us?"

"Nina says that dream catcher pentagram will keep her from changing into a werewolf."

"Yeah, and I'm dating the homecoming queen."

"It's just around the bend," Wilma announced.

The path opened into a large clearing. The forest ringed a large lake.

"Here," Wilma said, pointing. "Deadman's Landing."

Deadman's Landing was a dilapidated pier that jutted twenty yards into the water. The wooden pier rested on barrel floats. Broken, splintered boards ran the length of the pier. Anyone brave enough to venture upon it would be taking his life in his hands indeed. The pier bobbed and swayed with the slow rolling of the lake's waves.

The lake itself was mirror black. A cool breeze swam from off the surface, chilling the onlookers. They walked to the water's edge.

"I'd hate to think what lies beneath that surface," Bob said.

"Some say it is bottomless," Wilma said.

"What did you want to show us?" Nina said to Wilma.

Wilma walked to the edge of the treeline. "Here." She pointed to the ground.

"What is it?" Joe asked.

"Looks just like the dream catcher," Nina replied.

Water-smoothed stones formed a circle two feet

in diameter. Sticks and twigs were laid out at angles that mirrored the intricate weaving of the dream catcher Nina wore around her neck. The open center was the same pentagram.

"Here is where I taught my son the Ocala legends. Here is where he heard the ancient stories."

"What stories?" Bob asked.

"About skinwalkers."

"Werewolves?"

"You call them werewolves. We call them skinwalkers."

"What are you talking about?" Gayle said.

"Each country has a legend about people being able to change into various animals," Nina explained. "In some countries, the skinwalker, or shape-shifter, is evil. That's what's confusing about John Winokea and his shape-shifting: Traditionally, Native Americans never changed into an animal for evil purposes, but to become one with the animal and nature."

"Maybe," Bob added, "John's interest in shape-shifting made him vulnerable to the spirit of the Wolf Man from the movie."

"Yeah," Joe continued, "each monster seeks out something similar, something it knows, and then becomes a part of that. Like Count Dracula seeking out the Carfax Hotel and Mina, his lost love."

"Well," Nina said, "at least that's the theory. So far, our theories haven't exactly been *exact*. At least with Count Dracula, we had a clearer understanding of what to do. This time, we're dealing with flesh-and-blood people."

"I don't know what any of you are talking about," Gayle said. "I just want to find Don and end all of this."

"So, what do we do now?" Joe said.

"Now we wait," said Wilma.

They looked around the darkened clearing. Nina switched on the flashlight she had taken from the trunk of her car. Joe held the camcorder up and checked the strength of the battery. He was glad it was fully charged.

Wilma sat at the edge of the small circle of stones. She rubbed out the pentagram and the image of the wolf. Then she drew a circle in the dirt, with a series of bisecting lines in the center.

The waning full moon rose over the tops of the trees on the other side of the lake. Over the mirror of black water, it looked like there were two full moons: one in the sky and the other sitting atop the dark water.

Crickets chanted. The rustle of leaves — whether caused by the wind or by nocturnal creatures awakening to the night — provided a steady beat for the chorus of crickets.

"Let's wait over here," Joe suggested. He moved to the edge of the clearing, the camcorder ready.

Bob followed him, the wolfbane held tightly in

his hand. The wolfbane would subdue the were-wolf, but what if the camera didn't work? What would they do next? He patted the leather belt with the large silver buckle he had wrapped around him under his shirt. He had to conceal it because he had "borrowed" it from Gayle's house hours earlier. If the wolfbane failed and the camera failed, Bob intended to use the heavy silver buckle against the werewolf.

A hot wind brushed the back of Bob's neck. He reached back and rubbed the back of his neck. The hot air hit his hand. It felt as though he were standing too close to a fire.

Bob turned. He was staring at a large hairy chest. He looked up into the luminous bloodred eyes of a werewolf. The werewolf's head was pointed down, exhaling hot, putrid breath into Bob's face.

Bob took a step back and he thrust the wolfbane in front of him. "Dude, your mouthwash ain't making it."

"What?" Joe said. Then he, too, saw the werewolf.

The creature growled and struck out at Bob. He ducked, and the daggerlike claws caught the top of his head, slapping off the black yacht cap. One of the claws hooked into the cap, shredding it into little pieces.

"NO!" Bob screamed. He jumped at the werewolf, pressing the wolfbane against the large hairy chest. A hissing sound filled the air, as did the acrid smell of burning hair and flesh.

The werewolf howled in pain. He smacked Bob's arm away. Bob reeled and fell to the ground. A fiery shower of pain whipped through his arm. The wolfbane fell from his hand.

"Got 'em!" Joe shouted above the snapping and growling. He pointed the camera at the werewolf, flipped open the preview screen, and began filming.

Nothing happened. The camera was running, the tape was winding forward, but all the screen showed was the werewolf stepping toward Joe.

"Run, Joe!" Nina yelled.

Joe lowered the camera just as the werewolf struck him across the shoulder. He slammed into the ground, and the camera bounced away from him.

The werewolf bolted toward Nina. She lifted her dream catcher, but not in time. The werewolf easily lifted her from the ground and disappeared with her back into the woods.

Nina's screams filled the dark night air.

And then all was silent.

CHAPTER SEVENTEEN

Joe felt as though his lungs were going to burst. He heard the heavy panting of Bob behind him. He didn't know what had happened to Gayle or Wilma. All he knew was, they had to find Nina.

The forest was dark and deep. Visibility was limited to a few yards in front of them. He couldn't see the werewolf, but he could hear the monster crashing through the brush in front of them.

They kept running. But after a few more yards, Joe realized that he could no longer hear the werewolf ahead of them.

"Stop!" he yelled, coming to a sudden halt.

Bob stumbled, trying to avoid colliding with Joe.

"What's wrong?" Bob said, panting and wheezing.

"Listen," Joe said softly, gulping in air as quietly as possible.

"What?" Bob said, wheezing.

"Shhh!"

The forest was silent. No rustling of leaves or brush. No crickets. No hooting of night owls. Just silence. Unnatural silence.

"Where's Gayle?" Joe asked in a whisper.

"I don't know," Bob panted. He doubled over. "I think I'm going to be sick."

A warm breeze swept over him.

The large, hairy arm of the werewolf barely missed Bob as he bent over.

Joe lifted the camera and turned it on. "C'mon," Joe said. "Smile for the camera!" The werewolf swiped at Joe. He stumbled backward.

Bob had fallen to his knees. He pulled the wolfbane from his pocket and then whipped the leather belt with the heavy silver buckle from around his waist. He spun around, swinging the belt.

The silver buckle walloped the right side of the werewolf's head. The monster howled in torment. Bob swung the belt again, but the werewolf grabbed the leather end of the belt and yanked on it. Bob was jerked forward into the rock-hard chest of the werewolf. He bounced off and fell to the ground. The werewolf held the belt over its head and howled triumphantly.

Bob lay on his back, dazed, the wind knocked out of him. He shook his head. His eyes focused just in time to see the werewolf throw the belt into the thick brush. The monster reached down and lifted Bob with one hand, holding the teenager two feet from the ground. The monster's fetid, hot breath hit Bob like a furnace blast.

"Hey, dude," Bob said, struggling to release himself from the monster's grip. "You need to trim those nose hairs." He grabbed the werewolf by the jowls and held the monster's jaws at bay.

"The camera's not working!" Joe shouted from behind him. "It's not sucking him in. This isn't Wilma's son. It's Don!"

"I'm a little too busy to ponder theory with you right now, Joe. I could use some help here."

Joe put the camera down and ran to his friend. He dove into the monster's middle with a perfect shoulder tackle. The beast fell to the ground, with Bob landing smack on his face.

Joe and Bob began pummeling the werewolf with all their strength. The werewolf snapped and clawed at the duo. Joe grabbed it in a headlock.

"Where's your wolfbane?" Joe shouted.

"Oh, yeah!" Bob responded. He reached into his shirt pocket and pulled out the plant. He rubbed it into the werewolf's face.

The smell of burning fur filled the air. The werewolf howled in agony. The monster squirmed and twisted its head around, head-butting Joe.

Joe groaned and let go as he fought to stay conscious.

The werewolf flipped over on all fours and faced the two teenagers. Bob held the wolfbane in front of him. Joe stood on wobbly legs.

"Now what?" Bob said.

"Where's Nina?" Joe said, rubbing his forehead.

"Good question. This isn't right. But right now, let's focus on our immediate problem," Bob said, nodding at the monster.

The werewolf's fur stood on end. Its black lips were curled to reveal large, yellow teeth. Its hellish red eyes bore into the two boys. It snorted and growled.

"He wouldn't have just dropped Nina!" Joe shouted. For the first time since they had been friends, Bob heard genuine fear in Joe's voice.

The werewolf snapped at them. Bob thrust the wolfbane toward the beast, and the monster moved back.

"Wish I hadn't lost that silver buckle," Bob said.

A distant howl echoed throughout the forest. The wolf raised its head and listened. Then it turned and ran away from Joe and Bob, disappearing into the darkness of the forest.

"What was that all about?" Joe said.

"I don't know," Bob replied. "But we better find Nina. I've got a bad feeling about this, Joe."

"Me too."

A glint of light caught Bob's attention. He headed toward it and reached down to pick up Gayle's barrel racing championship buckle.

Again, a lone, distant howl filled the forest. It was soon joined by a chorus of howls.

Then a scream punctuated the night air. It was a scream of pain and terror that turned the boys' blood to ice.

"Nina!" Bob gasped.

CHAPTER EIGHTEEN

Bob and Joe ran in the direction of the scream. It was the same direction the werewolf had bolted. Moments later, they found themselves in a small clearing. The moonlight streamed through the trees and gave the forest floor a dark, bluish tint.

Two werewolves stood in the middle of the clearing. Nina lay between them, motionless.

Bob and Joe moved slowly toward the two hellhounds. Bob swung the belt with its heavy silver buckle like a pendulum. Joe wielded a large, broken tree limb he'd picked off the forest floor.

The two beasts sniffed the air as the boys edged closer. Then they lowered their heads, their hackles at attention.

Every muscle in Bob's body was a tightly coiled spring waiting to explode.

Nina groaned and moved her arm.

The werewolves turned their attention to the girl at their feet.

"No!" Bob screamed. He lunged at the bigger of the pair, swinging the belt buckle.

The heavy silver buckle caught the werewolf on the shoulder. The monster howled and fell.

The smaller werewolf leaped at Bob. Bob groaned as the werewolf slammed into him. They hit the ground, the werewolf nearly crushing him with its weight. The air burst from Bob's lungs, and he felt as though his whole body was about to collapse.

Joe swung his tree limb like a baseball bat and hit the werewolf across the right side of its head. The monster yelped in pain and rolled from Bob.

Joe was about to swing the limb again when the larger werewolf recovered from the blow and grabbed the limb, breaking it easily in two.

"No!" Joe yelled. He threw himself at the werewolf. They hit the ground hard and rolled for several feet. Joe ended up on top of the monster. He grabbed the beast by the throat. The werewolf squirmed as Joe tightened his grip. The monster grabbed Joe's wrists, squeezing them like a vise. It pushed Joe's hands away from him, and then tossed him to the side. Joe rolled and hit a tree. He did not move.

The larger werewolf trotted over to the smaller one. They greeted each other by nuzzling their muzzles.

Nina stirred, but the werewolves ignored her. She watched helplessly as the larger of the pair walked to Joe and turned him over. It was about to sink its teeth into Joe's flesh, to taste his warm, sweet blood, when something rustled in the brush behind it. The monster spun around.

Wilma Winokea stepped into the clearing, a small dream catcher in front of her. A soft chant came from her lips. She had no fear about her. She walked up to the werewolf, holding the dream catcher toward the beast.

Nina stood on wobbly legs, then helped Bob to stand.

Joe stood, shook his head to clear it, and joined his friends.

Wilma remained motionless. She continued chanting.

Both werewolves raised their hackles. They growled at the approaching shaman, snapping at her as she drew nearer.

But they seemed afraid to attack her. Wilma continued forward, still extending the dream catcher. The monsters began to back away. Their fur lay down and their growling ceased.

Nina's eyes were fixed on the shaman. She took her dream catcher from around her neck and held it forward, joining Wilma.

The werewolves whimpered and lay down. With their massive heads between their paws, they looked as though they had fallen asleep.

Nina watched as a gray mist rose around the monsters and began to surround them. Wilma continued chanting. She held a dream catcher over one beast and instinctively, Nina held hers over the other. The mist covered the two werewolves. The werewolves were starting to change — first losing their long canine snouts, then the ears. Fore and hind limbs became human legs and arms. Paws elongated into human fingers. Flesh-tearing teeth shrunk and disappeared behind the black lips. The black lips then gave way to pink flesh.

Don Earl and Gayle lay before them, peacefully sleeping.

"Neat trick," Bob said. He and Joe joined Wilma and Nina.

"We must get them back to the circle of stones," Wilma said. "It will protect them."

Nina knelt next to Gayle. The rodeo queen opened her eyes. "Don Earl," Gayle said softly. She reached out to her boyfriend.

"They are weak," Wilma said. "Their spirits are weak. We must quickly get them to the circle or the skinwalker's spirit will change them again."

Don Earl groaned. "What happened? Where am I?"

"We don't have time to explain," Joe said. "Besides, I don't think you're going to believe us when we tell you."

They helped the couple to stand.

"The dream catcher stopped the spirit of the skinwalker, didn't it?" Nina asked Wilma

Wilma smiled. "You have the spirit of the

shaman," the old woman said. "Perhaps you will be my pupil."

"My hat is gone," Bob said, a quiver in his voice. He turned from the group, brushing his eyes.

"At least we're still in one piece," Joe said, placing a hand on his friend's shoulder. He flipped on the camera. It came to life. "This should have worked."

"What now?" Bob said as he turned back to the group.

"We must return to the black water and destroy the skinwalker," Wilma said, and she turned and walked away.

"But he's your son," Nina said, following. "There's got to be another way."

"He is not my son anymore. My son could never turn these innocent children into killers. The skinwalker has killed my son," Wilma said with determination. "And now we must kill the skinwalker!"

CHAPTER NINETEEN

"That was Gayle we fought," Joe said to Bob as they neared the circle of stones. "She must have changed into a werewolf and followed us. She was distracting us from Don and Nina."

"I know you're not going to understand this," Nina said to Don and Gayle. "But you've got to remain in the circle. If you don't, you'll transform into werewolves again."

"We'll explain later," Joe said. "Just trust us."

Gayle leaned against Don. She was too weak to talk and had been easy to lead back to the edge of the black lake.

"They must remain within the circle until we have destroyed the skinwalker," Wilma said.

Don and Gayle stepped into the circle and lay down. Both were soon fast asleep.

Then Wilma said softly:

> *"The way you walked was thorny —*
> *Through no fault of your own.*

> *But as the rain enters the soil,*
> *The rivers enter the sea,*
> *So tears run to a predestined end.*
> *Your suffering is over.*
> *Now you will find peace for eternity."*

"There she goes again," Bob whispered to the other two. "Has her voice changed?"

"Yeah," Joe said. "It's like she has a foreign accent now."

"You know what, guys?" Nina said. "I just thought of something. Something I heard a long time ago: Sometimes the simplest answer *is* the right answer. We've really complicated this, haven't we?"

Bob turned to Joe. "Do you know what she's talking about?"

Joe shrugged.

"Something has been nagging at me since we got here, since we met Wilma. At first, I thought it was because she was so spiritual, you know, chanting and talking about the dream catcher and all. But you know what? I wasn't hearing Wilma. I was hearing the old gypsy woman from *The Wolf Man.*"

"I think you got hit too hard in the head," Bob said.

"I'm not crazy," Nina said. "Not yet, anyway."

"You mean Maleva, don't you?" Joe said. "The fortune-teller's mother from the movie."

"Yeah," Nina replied. "All this time we've been

after Don Earl and John Winokea. But they haven't been the problem at all. Or at least not the root of it." Nina turned to look at Wilma. Bob and Joe followed her gaze.

Wilma was staring into the circle of stones. "The werewolf is from an ancient and noble race who taught humans language and culture," she said softly, as if speaking to herself. "But humans turned on the werewolves, driving them deep into the forests and caves, where they reverted into the monsters of humankind's darkest and deepest fears. They were hunted by humans and so began hunting humans, cursing the human blood."

"What's she talking about?" Bob said.

"The werewolf legend," Joe said. Then he whispered to his friend, "She's stopped calling them skinwalkers. Her voice has definitely changed. It's not American anymore. It's European."

Bob's eyes widened. "Yeah," he whispered. "You're right."

"The ancient ones wanted these two to join them," Wilma said, nodding toward Don and Gayle.

"And so shall you all," said a deep voice from behind them.

Nina, Bob, and Joe spun around. Deputy Barnes stood behind them, his gun pointing at one and then the others.

"What?" Bob said.

"Just another country bumpkin," the deputy said

with a smirk. He took off his thick glasses. "You didn't tell them, did you, *Mother?*"

Bob and Joe looked at Wilma and then at the deputy.

"You're John Winokea?" Bob said.

Chad snorted. "I'm Chad Barnes — Wilma's son from her first marriage."

"You're an Ocala, too?" Joe said.

"Of course."

"And a member of the Elder Council?" Bob said.

"Yep."

"Should have known," Bob said.

"Why?" Chad said. "Why should you have known?"

"We should have known we couldn't count on you, Chad," Bob said. "No one's as dumb as you played it."

"*You* were dumb enough to believe me." Chad smiled.

Bob raised the belt and buckle.

"Uh-uh-uh," Chad said, pointing the pistol at Bob. "I'll drop you like a bad habit before you have a chance to swing that thing."

"But you don't have any bullets in your gun, re-member?" Bob took a step forward.

Chad raised the gun into the air and squeezed the trigger. The gun exploded and a flash of fire shot out of the barrel.

Wilma sat by the circle, unmoving, chanting and holding forth the dream catcher.

"All your talk of movie monsters coming to life is pure fiction," Chad said. "We have been skinwalkers for years, waiting until the right time to come forth and reclaim what was once ours."

"We?" Nina said.

The heavy thud of footfalls and cracking limbs and crumbling leaves echoed in the forest. And then two giant werewolves emerged.

"My little half brother, John, was believed to be the leader," Chad said, pointing with the pistol at the grayish werewolf. "Of course, you might have thought the sheriff there would be the leader." Chad pointed the pistol at the dark werewolf. "Who would have suspected that a half-blind country bumpkin would actually be the leader?"

"So, um, what about that skinwalker stuff?" Bob asked.

"All cultures have shape-shifting legends," Chad replied, grinning. "All legends have a basis in fact. A little truth here, a little truth there. The real truth is that we're not some made-up Hollywood monsters. We're as real as the blood that pumps through your veins." His voice deepened into a low growl. "The blood that I will drink from your body!"

Chad dropped to all fours as the transformation began. His gun fell to the forest floor beside him. Joe made a move toward the pistol, but the other two werewolves snarled and snapped their teeth, warning the teen away.

Chad's body twisted. His eyes rolled back into his head. His head snapped as the bones of his jaw cracked and pushed forward. His lower teeth grew longer and longer until they jutted over his upper lip. His ears pushed out from his head, growing longer and pointed. Thick dark fur snaked from every pore of his skin.

His back arched as his body stretched. Arms and legs become fore and hind limbs, and his hands were soon padded paws that encased long black claws.

The werewolf lifted its head to the bloodred moon and howled. Chad did not look like the other two werewolves. He was the Wolf Man. The Wolf Man legend from the movie and the ancient myth of the skinwalker had become one in Chad Barnes.

Joe desperately fidgeted with the camera. He didn't know what would happen when he turned it on the monster. Would just the spirit of the Wolf Man be sucked into the digital camera, or would Chad's soul also be captured forever on film — literally?

The Wolf Man straightened himself to his full seven-foot height. He seemed to be gathering all his strength. Then he lunged at the trio.

Bob was ready for him. He swung the belt, hitting the Wolf Man across the chest with the large silver buckle. The Wolf Man bellowed in pain.

Joe raised the camera and turned it on. He flipped open the preview screen, watching nervously as the Wolf Man moved slowly toward him. The camera was on, it was recording, but nothing was happening.

The Wolf Man leaped at Bob, grabbing him by the throat. The monster clamped his furry hands around the soft flesh and squeezed.

Bob gagged, dropped the belt, and grabbed the wrists of the werewolf. He twisted the monster's wrists, but they were like steel. Bob tried to suck in air, but couldn't. Pin-sized flashes of light exploded around the edges of his vision. He was blacking out. His movements became slow and weak. He tried to swallow. His throat burned. His arms went limp. Soon he would be suffocated, dead.

"No!" Nina screamed. She picked up the belt and swung it at the Wolf Man. The heavy silver buckle slammed against the left side of the Wolf Man's head, and the beast crashed to the ground.

Nina suddenly felt a sharp pain in her right arm. Another werewolf had clamped down on her arm with its massive jaw. She screamed as the teeth tore her flesh and hit bone.

Joe dropped the camera and slammed into the werewolf that had Nina in its jaws. All three hit the ground. Joe hurled a roundhouse right into the werewolf's rib cage. The cracking of bone and cartilage echoed across the dark water. The werewolf howled, spitting up blood. Nina scrambled away, clutching her arm.

Joe raised his fist and aimed for the beast's jaw. The other werewolf growled and leaped at Joe, its enormous jaw open to reveal the large teeth that were headed straight for Joe's throat. But suddenly, it was jerked back in midair.

"Not today, fuzzy butt!" Bob yelled. He had the belt looped around the werewolf's throat.

The Wolf Man shook his head and stood. Blood oozed out of the gash on the side of his head. He moved slowly but with determination. He grabbed Bob by the shoulders and lifted him off the werewolf.

Joe jumped at the Wolf Man, desperate to rescue his friend. The monster threw Bob right at him. The two teens slammed into each other and hit the ground with a thud.

Nina knelt down by her friends, pressing against the wound on her arm, blood seeping through her fingers.

"This is not like Dracula," she said, panting. "This is real. These are real werewolves. We're gonna die."

Bob groaned. "Joe."

Joe rolled over and sat up. He shook his head. "Not yet, buddy. They haven't won yet."

Bob picked up the belt. Joe grabbed the camera.

Then they all stood together — Nina, Joe, and Bob — and faced the Wolf Man and his two companions.

"Maybe today is a good day to die," Bob said.

Nina sighed. "I really hate you quoting old movies like that. Can't you think of anything a little more positive to say at a moment like this?"

"Now or never, boys and girls," Joe said. He smiled at his friends.

Bob raised the belt above his head and dashed at the Wolf Man.

The Wolf Man caught the buckle in his hand and jerked on the belt. Bob stumbled to the ground. All three monsters had surrounded him before Joe and Nina could move. Bob screamed as he stared into three pairs of luminous bloodred eyes and saw three sets of razor-sharp fangs aiming for his throat.

Joe dove into the fray. He grabbed one werewolf and body-slammed him to the ground. The werewolf groaned and lay still.

Nina managed to pick the belt up from the fray. She whopped the gray werewolf on the side of the head. He, too, hit the ground and did not move.

The Wolf Man stood in a crouching position, growling, his claws up, ready to slice anyone who came near him.

Bob scooted and scrambled to his feet. He joined his two friends.

"It's just you now, dog breath," Joe said.

"C'mon," Bob added, "we've got your leash right here."

"This isn't the time for fancy one-liners, guys," Nina said through gritted teeth.

The Wolf Man straightened to his full height and

WOLF MAN™

turned his face up to the sky. He howled at the bloodred moon sitting at its zenith.

Then he jerked his head down and barked. The sound was explosive, and it sent a searing wind at the three teens. Nina, Joe, and Bob hit the ground, stunned.

The Wolf Man crept over to the prone teens. He howled again.

Wilma stood. She removed her pentagram dream catcher from around her neck and tossed it at the Wolf Man. The silver hoop hit the monster in the chest and stuck there. The air was filled first with the acrid smell of burnt fur and flesh and then with the horrible cry of the werewolf.

The monster staggered backward, toward the water's edge. In a matter of moments, the other two wolves were transformed where they lay, back into the human forms of John Winokea and Sheriff Marshall.

Joe scrambled to his feet, grabbed the camera, and moved quickly toward the monster. He raised the camera and pointed it at the Wolf Man. He watched on the small screen as the werewolf howled in pain and torment as the dream catcher burned into his flesh. The monster teetered on the water's edge and finally fell into the black liquid. The water bubbled and boiled as the werewolf thrashed about, struggling to pull the dream catcher from his flesh. Smoke and small bursts of flame burst from the monster's paws.

Joe moved forward. Perhaps each monster was different. The Wolf Man definitely wasn't Dracula. Joe didn't know what would happen, but he wasn't going to stop filming.

Then just as suddenly, the werewolf stopped thrashing about and screaming. He lay still. Joe watched through the viewfinder as the werewolf shrunk and took the shape of a man — Chad Barnes, son of Wilma Winokea and deputy sheriff of the town of Wales.

But that was it. Nothing else happened. Joe pressed the STOP button. He hit REWIND. If it had worked, he would see the Wolf Man in the preview screen, just as he had seen Dracula.

Joe stopped the rewind. He took a deep breath. He hit PLAY.

"Well?" Bob said.

"It's the same," Joe said, puzzled. "The Wolf Man's not here. Just Wilma's son dying."

"Joe," Nina said softly. "Stop."

Joe hit the STOP button. He turned. He gasped when he saw Wilma standing in the circle of stone, an evil smile on her face.

Bob snapped his fingers. "That's it." He turned to his friends. "Remember in *The Wolf Man:* It all started with the old gypsy woman, the mother of the werewolf that had attacked Larry Talbot. She knew that her son was a werewolf all along. She *knew* that anyone with the image of the pentagram on him would be killed by the werewolf. She *knew*

the secret all along and yet she did nothing to stop him."

"But Wilma helped us. She made the dream catchers. She helped Gayle. She led us here —" Nina began.

But Joe cut her off. "She led us here, all right. To our deaths!"

Nina stared at the old shaman. "I believed in you," she said slowly.

Wilma laughed. "You have some gifts, but you are too trusting, child. You still have much to learn about the way of the spirits — that the good and the evil are not always separated so neatly."

Joe had seen enough. He raised the camera and punched the RECORD button.

"No, Joe," Nina said calmly. She was still gazing at Wilma. "That won't work. Not this time. Not by itself. We need science *and* magic this time."

Wilma rose in the air, hovering above the circle of stones. But she was no longer Wilma. She was Maleva the Gypsy from *The Wolf Man*.

"Give me the camera," Nina ordered.

Joe handed her the camera. Nina pulled the last of the coarse string from her front pocket and used it to tie the dream catcher to the lens of the camera. She looked at the preview screen. With the dream catcher in front of the lens, the pentagram outline showed in the preview screen.

Nina pointed the camera at the levitating Wilma. Beams of light shot out from the dream catcher camcorder and struck Wilma, halting her ascent. The old woman spun, slowly at first and then faster and faster until she became a blur of gray and black and white in the dull colorless light of the full moon.

The whirlwind of grays and blacks and whites swept toward the lifeless body of Chad Barnes, still floating in the black water. The whirlwind struck the body and enveloped it. The body was consumed, becoming part of the whirlwind.

The whirlwind rose, and the spinning increased. It rustled the leaves and brush of the forest and rippled the black water. A loud suction noise filled the air, and the swirling mass of grays and blacks and whites was pulled into the center of the dream catcher, into the camera's lens. Wilma Winokea and her werewolf son disappeared.

And then the forest was quiet. The waning full moon hung in the sky, oblivious to the horrors and terrors it had prompted.

Nina walked over to the circle of stones and sat down. She untied the dream catcher from the camera and placed it in the circle. She handed the camera back to Joe. "Tape this, Joe."

Joe took the camera and raised it to his eye. He pushed the RECORD button. He zoomed in on the talisman on the ground.

Then Nina said softly,

"The way you walked was thorny —
Through no fault of your own.

WOLF MAN™

But as the rain enters the soil,
The rivers enter the sea,
So tears run to a predestined end.
Your suffering is over.
Now you will find peace for eternity."

The dream catcher vanished.
The night was at peace.

CHAPTER TWENTY
Sunday Afternoon, 1 P.M.
Gayle's Dining Room

"I didn't realize I was so hungry," Don Earl said as he bit into a slice of toast. He had already eaten half a loaf of toasted bread and nearly a whole jar of strawberry jam. He munched on the bread and then gulped down a large glass of orange juice.

"Can I get you anything else?" Gayle asked.

"No. Thank you," he said with a smile. He leaned over and kissed her on the cheek. "Hey!" he shouted as Snow jumped up and tried to crawl into his lap. "You're too big, you jealous baby."

"She just wants to be loved," Gayle said.

"Yeah, after all," Bob said as he chewed on a piece of bacon, "you did devour her. Remember?"

"No, I don't remember," Don Earl said. "And I don't know if I believe you or not. I don't know what to believe."

"It's true," Joe said. He sat across from Don and Gayle, next to Bob. He turned to his friend. "Don't eat with your mouth full."

"I'm hungry, too," Bob protested.

"It's one thing to be hungry," Nina began, "it's another to be rude."

"Well, I don't believe I ate meat," Don Earl said. "I haven't eaten meat in ten years. It's cruel."

Bob look skeptically at the young cowboy. "I find it hard to believe that you don't eat meat, but you do ride bulls."

"Hey," Don said, "like I always say: I just ride 'em; I don't eat 'em."

"I'm glad my parents haven't woken up yet," Gayle said. "I don't know how I'm going to explain all of this."

"Sometimes it's better to just shrug your shoulders and say, 'I don't know' or 'I don't recall,'" Captain Bob said.

"That proves it," Nina said. "You're going to be a politician."

The others laughed.

"Now, let me see if I have this right," Don began. "Wilma and her first son were really the old gypsy woman and her son from an old movie called *The Wolf Man*. Right?"

"Yeah," Bob said, his mouth full of toast. Crumbs fell over his shirt.

"Can't take this boy anywhere," Nina said with a deep sigh.

"All of this happened because you guys released some monsters from some old movies? Is that right?" Don Earl looked genuinely puzzled.

"Yes," Joe said.

"We swear," Nina added.

Don Earl shook his head. "I think y'all been drinking salt water and getting too much sun on the beach."

"Don," Gayle said seriously. "You don't think I'm crazy, do you? I saw you change into a werewolf."

"Hmm," Don said as he rubbed his chin. "I always wanted to know what I looked like with a full beard."

"I like you just the way you are," Gayle said. She quickly kissed his cheek. "Smooth skin, vegetarian, and all."

"We've got to go," Nina said. "Thanks for breakfast or lunch or whatever it was. I was starving. Fighting monsters always makes me hungry, and there was nothing at the biological station."

"Yeah, thanks," Bob said, standing up.

"Me, too," said Joe.

Don and Gayle walked the trio to Nina's Camaro.

"You know," Don said, "I had a dream last night of running through the woods like a dog."

"Let's hope it remains a dream," Joe said.

"I don't understand," Gayle said. "What did the skinwalker legend and the dream catcher have to do with *The Wolf Man?*"

"Only thing I can figure," Joe said, "is that each monster is different. With Dracula, it was just him. But with the Wolf Man, it was both the monster and his mother."

"And apparently," Nina said, "their spirits or essences, or whatever you want to call it, were drawn to the Ocala skinwalker legends."

"But we've known Wilma and Deputy Barnes for years," Gayle said. "You mean, they've just up and disappeared? They don't exist anymore?"

"We drove by Wilma's house before we came here," Nina explained. "The place hasn't been lived in for at least twenty years."

"Yeah," Bob said. "The place is falling down."

Gayle shuttered. "I'm getting cold shivers just thinking about it. This is like something out of a horror movie."

"That's the point we're trying to make," Bob said with a big toothy grin.

"But now they're safely put away," Joe added, patting the small digital stick he carried in his front pocket.

"What would have happened if you hadn't captured the Wolf Man and his mother in the camera?" Gayle said.

"We'd all be werewolves," Joe said. He patted Don on the shoulder. "And Mr. Vegetarian here would probably be enjoying a nice tenderloin right now."

"Yeech." Don Earl shuddered.

Gayle looked at Nina. "I still don't understand about Wilma. Why did she try to help us if she was really evil?"

Nina looked troubled. "I'm still not sure, either,"

she admitted. "I think she was like Maleva the gypsy from the movie — she was torn between love for her son and doing what was right. I still think, in her own way, she tried to help us."

Gayle nodded. "I believe that, too." The two girls locked eyes and smiled.

"All right, enough with the serious, mystical stuff already. I call shotgun!" Bob said. He ran to the convertible.

"Oh no, you don't!" Joe shouted. He reached out with a long arm and pulled his shorter friend back. Joe opened the passenger door and hopped in the front seat.

"One of these days, you're going to wish you hadn't done that," Bob said. He walked around to the other side of the car and crawled into the back-seat.

"I'll hold my breath until then," Joe said. "In the meantime, you can thank me for this." Joe twisted the latch on the glove compartment. He took out a faded, tattered black object and flipped it to Bob.

"My hat!" he shouted. He hugged the old yacht captain's hat and then tugged it down tightly on his head. *"I'm off, said the mad man.* Thanks, buddy!" He slapped Joe on the shoulder.

"Yeah, thanks," Nina said as she climbed into the driver's seat and started up the car. She adjusted the rearview mirror. Captain Bob was sitting in the back, a big smile on his face, the hat firmly on his head. She fought back a smile. She was happy that

Bob had gotten his beloved hat back, but she wasn't going to let him know that.

"Y'all drive carefully," Don Earl said.

"Bye," Gayle added.

"Thanks," Nina said, and she pushed the lever into drive and nosed the car out of the driveway.

They were just outside of the Wales city limits when Bob suddenly bolted up.

"Oh, no!" he shouted.

"What?" a startled Nina said, her foot hitting the brake. The car screeched to a stop.

"I forgot to get any plants for my extra-credit project! Now Dr. James is going to fail me!" He fell back into the seat and pulled the cap down over his eyes. "My mom's gonna kill me. Then she's going to make me stay home and do my homework every night."

"You knew the job was dangerous when you took it," Nina said as she pressed on the accelerator.

"Don't worry, buddy," Joe said. "You can use the extra plants I have pressed at home. They're already keyed as well."

A smile formed on Bob's face. "Thanks, man."

Nina grabbed her CD case, flipped it open, and pulled out a silver disk. She slid it into the player and turned up the volume.

"Aw-right!" Bob shouted over the rushing wind and the loud music. "I *looove* Lynyrd Skynyrd!" Bob sat up in the seat and pretended to hold a microphone. *"Sweet home, Alabama!"* he screamed.

"Hey!" Joe shouted. "You're ruining a perfectly good song!"

"Critics!" Bob shouted back.

"Uh-oh, guys," Nina said. She turned down the CD player.

"What? Why'd you stop the song, man?" Bob asked.

"Look," Nina said. Her voice was almost a gasp. Her eyes were wide with fear.

Joe and Bob turned around. Twenty yards behind the Camaro was a battered old 1964 Chevy step-side pickup truck, painted black and white with canned spray paint. A red police siren with BB dimples sat atop the hood.

Deputy Chad Barnes sat behind the wheel of the police prowl truck. Wilma Winokea, his mother, sat in the passenger seat.

"How is this possible?" Bob shouted. "This can't be real!"

"Oh, it's real, all right," Nina said. "As real as classic movie monsters coming to life."

"This is unbelievable," Joe said. He checked his shirt pocket. The digital video stick was still there.

The truck edged closer. Chad and Wilma stared at the trio and smiled. Evil smiles. Smiles that said not a word but spoke volumes nonetheless.

"Let's get out of here!" Bob said. "What does this car have in it, a hamster?"

"Hardly," Nina said. She stomped on the accelerator. The car lurched forward, a high-pitched, high-performance whine piercing the air. The engine roared as the Camaro shifted into high gear. The car jetted down the highway.

Bob watched as the truck became little more than a dot on the horizon.

He turned around and sat squarely in the seat. He glanced over Nina's shoulder. She hadn't slowed down yet. The speedometer needle was slowly sweeping past eighty-five. Normally, Bob would be scared to death to go faster than fifty-five, but he made an exception this time and settled back into the seat. He didn't care if Nina drove one hundred miles per hour all the way back to San Tomas Inlet. Just as long as they got away from Wales and its werewolves.

EPILOGUE
Two Weeks Later
Hallway, Ponce de Leon High School

"Well?" Joe asked as he walked up to Captain Bob.

Bob was at his locker, fighting with the combination. After several tries, he jerked the locker opened. "D-plus."

"D-plus! Dr. James gave you a D-plus!" Joe shook his head. "I worked hard on that plant project."

"Yeah. That's what Dr. James said."

"What did Dr. James say?"

"That you worked hard on keying the plants."

"How did he know that I keyed the plants?"

Bob slammed his locker shut. "He recognized your handwriting."

Joe sighed. "You didn't rewrite the keys that I had written?"

"I didn't have time."

"You had two weeks."

"I've had to work at the Beach Burger. Plus I was busy with other things."

"Like what?"

"I downloaded that new game from the web."

"What new game?"

"*Dark Blood*. You know, the one about monsters."

"The next time you're on the Internet," Joe said as they walked down the hallway, "you ought to download some common sense."

"Yeah. I know," Bob said. "You figure out why we saw Wilma and Deputy Barnes?"

"I've watched *The Wolf Man* so many times I can recite all the lines blindfolded. The old gypsy woman and her son are in the movie."

"And we saw them disappear into the camera through the pentagram," Bob said.

"I know. I was there, remember? I even did a binary-code check. Everything is in place. I can't explain it."

"I've been thinking about it," Bob said slowly. "Chad and Wilma were real people before we released the Wolf Man from the movie. And they were bad people. So even after we captured the Wolf Man and his mother on film, Chad and Wilma are still out there. They're still skinwalkers."

Joe shook his head. "Better not tell Nina that theory. She'll want to go after them again. She took that spirit stuff pretty seriously."

They threw their skateboards on the ground and hopped on the decks. "I know," Bob said. He shoved Joe as he pushed off with his free foot. "Hey, I'll race ya!"

"Hey!" Joe yelled as he fought to keep his balance. He was soon skating after his friend.

Nina Nobriega's Home
Same Day

"Anybody home?" Mrs. Nobriega sat her briefcase down by the stairs and walked into the living room. "Hello, Nina. How was the bucky ball exam?" She sat in the winged-back Queen Anne chair opposite her daughter.

"Fine, Mom," Nina replied without looking up from the newspaper. "Mr. Cravens even liked my bucky ball balloon project. Believe it or not, Captain Bob helped me with it."

"Why wouldn't I believe it? Robert seems like a very nice young man."

Nina rolled her eyes and frowned at her mom. "You haven't seen him eat one of his peanut-butter-and-bologna sandwiches yet."

"Robert's just a growing young man, Nina."

"*Please*, Mother," Nina responded with a huff. "Don't use the word *man* and *Robert* in the same sentence." Then she smiled. "Unless, of course, you're providing an example of an oxymoron."

"Nina, remember what your grandmother used to say."

Nina sighed with resignation. Yes, she remembered what her grandmother always said. Her grandmother had been raised to be a proper southern lady and she tried to pass on her genteel manners to her granddaughter. When Nina was a little girl and would say something honest, her grandmother would always say, "Don't be ugly, dear."

"I've been meaning to ask you something."

Nina put the paper in her lap and looked at her mother. "Yes?"

"Well, your dad tried to use the camcorder last weekend, but when he played it back, all he got was images of swirling grays, blacks, and whites. Do you know anything about it?"

"Well," Nina began, "I let Joe use it. Maybe he and Bob did something to it."

"I don't mind you letting your friends use it; I just wish they wouldn't change all the adjustments."

"I'll call Joe and have him come over and fix it," Nina said with a smile. "Okay?"

"Okay. But tell him he better not try to fix anything else around here." Nina's mom left the room.

Nina sighed. She wondered if telling only half the truth was like telling a lie. It was a question she would pose to her philosophy teacher.

She returned her attention to the *San Tomas Inlet Interviewer* comic section and finished reading her favorite cartoon strip. Then she flipped through the rest of the paper. Not much else held her interest. Until she came to a small item in the police report:

Authorities are still perplexed as to the reason behind the vandalism. Several headstones were overturned and some of the crypts were broken into.

Police have denied that the vandalism has anything to do with the vampire cult investigation of two months ago or any connection to the recent theft of a brain from the School of Medicine at the University of Miami's San Tomas Inlet Extension campus. . . .

Missing brain? Nina thought. *Who would want to steal a brain?* She chuckled to herself.

But just as quickly, the smile dropped from her face. Only one answer popped into her mind: *Dr. Frankenstein.*

About the Author

Since childhood, Larry Mike Garmon has been an aficionado of things that go bump in the night. Watching such classic horror movies as *Frankenstein* and *Psycho* added to his anxiety about strangers with glowing eyes. Reading horror comic books and tales of terror from Edgar Allan Poe, Nathaniel Hawthorne, H. P. Lovecraft, and Ambrose Bierce compounded his concern, but also encouraged him to try writing scary stories of his own. He often listens to Bach and Metallica while writing his creepiest scenes.

Larry Mike lives with his wife, Nadezhda, in Altus, Oklahoma. They have five children — three grown and two still in school. Larry Mike is an English teacher at Altus High School, while Nadezhda is a pianist and vocalist. They have two dogs, two cats, and a vintage 1965 Buick Wildcat.

Although Larry Mike still enjoys a good horror movie or novel, he says there is nothing more horrifying than teaching a room full of teenagers! He is an active member of the Honor Writers Association, and can be reached at MonsterMan@LarryMike. com.